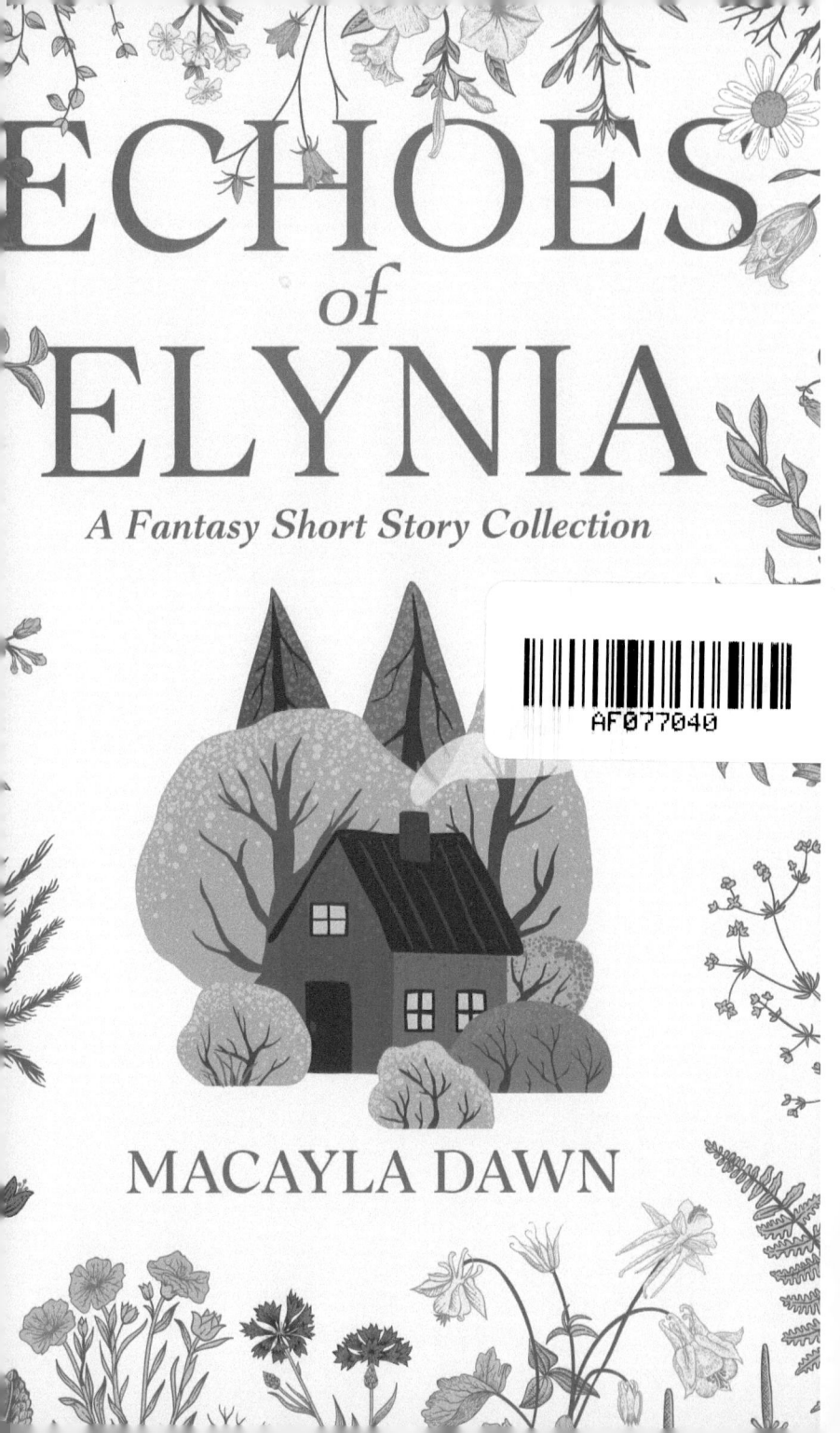

MACAYLA DAWN

Echoes of Elynia

First published by Self-Published 2025

Copyright © 2025 by Macayla Dawn

All rights reserved. No part of this publication may be reproduced, stored or transmitted in any form or by any means, electronic, mechanical, photocopying, recording, scanning, or otherwise without written permission from the publisher. It is illegal to copy this book, post it to a website, or distribute it by any other means without permission.

This novel is entirely a work of fiction. The names, characters and incidents portrayed in it are the work of the author's imagination. Any resemblance to actual persons, living or dead, events or localities is entirely coincidental.

First edition

ISBN: 979-8-3484-6290-1

This book was professionally typeset on Reedsy. Find out more at reedsy.com

For those who've never felt like they belong -

Elynia is for you.

Contents

ECHOES of ELYNIA	ii
WHISPERS OF ASH	1
WHAT ONCE WAS OURS	8
FORSAKEN ROOTS	16
WEIGHTED WINGS	23
MY RIVER'S EMBRACE	33
LOST FRAGMENTS	39
TANGLED PATH	46
UNWOVEN CHAINS	52
SHATTERED BLAME	59
GLIMPSES OF FROST	67
Sneak Peek...	74
The Mountain's Crown	75
ONE	77
TWO	78
THREE	83
Acknowledgments	89
About the Author	91
Also by Macayla Dawn	93

ECHOES of ELYNIA

WHISPERS OF ASH

I thought death would be painless. I assumed the world around me would cease to exist before I did. I hoped I would be an everlasting flame - snuffed out only when our oxygen finally evaporated, when resources eventually ran out, when the magical wells of Elynia suddenly ran dry.

Instead I'm stuck here, nearly dormant. I am acutely aware of every crackle of my being, every distant hum coming from my internal dwelling place. Though I am the heart of this cottage, it isn't enough to keep me going. Once, I blazed with certainty - with fervor. I danced, flicking shadows along the wooden walls, reaching high to the stone ceiling within this safe space, knowing I would be contained no matter how consuming I became.

Only faint embers remain of me now. I can no longer hold onto the life that was gifted to me out of love. I am no longer an anchor of light and hope. I am no more than a dying bed of elements thrown together by will. There is nothing I can do but succumb to the sleep calling to me. Nothing I can do, but wait.

Our cottage sits still in the heavy silence of winter. Though I have never experienced the cold touch of snow myself, I have heard it is like a numbing caress - one that leaves you breathless but longing for more. Snow does not yet pile along the ground, shifting itself in order to mound in front of the tall windows. Rather, it falls in a light flurry, contrasting against the dusk sky. A cold breeze drifts in from the open glass, heavy navy curtains fluttering in the wind, causing me to shudder under its wrath. Winter's bitter touch will surely speed along my death.

Though the world outside is frozen in a hushed embrace, inside, there is only the glow of what once was. The shelves placed delicately and intentionally within our one-room cottage are lined with ancient trinkets and crystals. The large maroon bed where our Makers often lie is untouched. It's been hours since they departed - a day I have spent waiting for them to return. Would they arrive in time to breathe me back to life?

In the far corner of our room, curled up in the seat of a rocking chair older than Elynia itself, a long, narrow shadow moves. My longest friend, my only companion. Though we cannot speak to each other using words, we communicate clearly. Though we cannot touch nor comfort each other, we share a bond far beyond what this world would have for us.

The ice fox. She is no ordinary creature, but one could say the same of me. A being of ice and winter herself, her fur shimmers like the light of a full moon, the faintest hint of frost clinging to her long tail. Eyes alive with quiet intelligence, they glow coldly, reflecting my own evaporating warmth back to me.

The house creaks as she stretches, choosing to jump from the chair with quiet ease, padding across the room to me. Her paws hardly touch the ground, leaving the illusion she is merely made of snowflakes flowing from a breeze.

As she pauses in her stance, she takes me in, gazing toward my still hearth. She's drawn to me in this moment, my fading heat allowing her to get closer than she's ever been. The air grows colder with every passing minute, suffocating me. She steps even closer, her slow breathing visible in the cool air as my flicker slows. It worries me to think of the inevitable - her being without me.

We've never known this world without the other. Our Makers created us in tandem - a gift to each other at their mating. As they embraced the other's figure, their gentle fingers caressing pointed ears and immortal features, they breathed vows of truth and promise to the other. Ceraphina departed with a single piece of her life force, creating me to warm their house and keep them alive. Eirwen did the same, gifting his lover with the ice fox to symbolize eternal care and curiosity of his partner.

Or so the story goes.

The ice fox, whom they nicknamed "Keeks", and I were not present before our creation. Our Makers often lay wrapped up in each other on their bed, retelling the story of the love from which we came. Their kind has surely died off, they've expressed, war forcing them into this hidden life they hold. The phrase *"it is but you and I"* is frequently repeated within this space, reminding me constantly I will never have someone to hold as they do.

Though Keeks and I are similar in a way, we will never be one as they are. She will never know how it feels to be captive and only observe the world around, and I will never understand the freedom she has - able to wander near and far - but still choose to return at the end of the day.

I know if I could leave, I would not choose to return.
There is too much to see.

Our Makers have never been gone this long. Everyday they leave to harvest, hunt, to search for others like them left in Elynia. I had begun to think myself eternal like them, my creation stretching back longer than we could possibly remember, but perhaps my thoughts were too generous. My subconscious flickers in and out - black fading the edges of my dark flame.

At first, all I knew was warmth. I was a surge - crackling, popping, eager to reach out and touch the edges of the cage surrounding me. I frequently licked at the dark air of the cottage, and our Makers always tended to my needs. I was everything - light, heat, motion, life. In return, I provided for them: a place to come together and warm up after long days spent in the sharp cold, a space to heat their meals, a way to boil their water. I was happy in my stone confinement - content to sit and hear the stories of their long lives.

Keeks was given free reign of the world around us, but she always reenters the cottage as night arrives. I once believed myself to be better than her, for there was never a question of whether I would be there for them at dusk. I was constant - a sure thing. She was a wild card, one that I felt didn't care for our Makers as I did.

But as time progressed, I realized we were both given chains in our own unique way. On days my flame was less vibrant, Keeks would often stay in rather than venturing out. Though she's never told me as much, I think my flame becomes unbearable for her at times.

Ice can only take so much heat before it melts.

As time has passed, our Makers have grown lax in their care for both of us. I used to wonder if this was due to the nature of their relationship - if eternity became too much, even for them. Now, I believe something in Elynia is shifting. They talk more often of war - of beings like them hoping to rise up and conquer. They no longer have time to sit in my warmth, sing of better days, share stories of how they met and accepted that perfect bond between them. Instead, they chatter excitedly for days to come.

They have gained a sense of confidence that their current life may be changing for one even better.

Perhaps they no longer need me. My crackling has slowed to nothing but a gentle murmur - whispers of ash. My heat drains from me, a bitter taste of embers is all that is left. I will never feel the caress of a lover. I will never sit in the presence of Keeks again in companionable silence. I will never experience walls outside this cottage.

A sharp shiver runs through me as Keeks paws at my cinders, jolting me from my inner defeat. She whines, urgency in her movements.

When did she get so close? Why would she risk her own life as I near the end of mine?

Just let the wind claim me. I will not belong to Elynia much longer.

But what am I, if not burning? I was not meant to dwindle. I am an aching fade and her presence is rushing the process along. With a single flame, I reach out to push her away, hoping to convey the uselessness of my situation. She cannot stoke my fire - she cannot provide what I need.

Her tail flicks against my flame, sending it back into myself. A small flurry drifts from her coat, reminding me of the open window hurrying along my demise. As if she understands my train of thought, her gaze traces back to the open pane.

Bouncing quickly to the top of the table beneath the glass, she uses her paws to push down the ledge of the window, closing it with all her might. The snow that had begun falling is now trapped behind the pane, just as I am trapped here, doomed to this fate. As she looks back at me, I see myself through the reflection of her sapphire eyes - weak, pathetic, no more than the flame of a match.

Stay there. Do not mourn for me.

She tilts her head, assessing my situation. I long to reassure her that this will be a better life for her with me gone - she will no longer have to run from our home to find safety and comfort. Perhaps our Makers will make another of her kind - gifting her a true friend. One that could understand her fully.

Keeks pads back to me, so effortless and graceful. She lays in front of me, as close as she can handle, yet still a remnant of my fever finds her figure. Water begins to puddle at her feet, dripping from the tips of her ears and nose. I attempt to pull myself back further - retreating into the very depths of my hearth, so as to not harm my friend.

I have accepted my fate. Our Makers will not return in time to heal me. I will never know if they will regret this - staying far away so long as to leave me behind permanently. I hope they did not come into trouble. I hope they did not find themselves trapped in these mountains without a fire to keep them warm. How I wish I could travel with them - a portable gift to keep them safe.

But that is not what they asked of me.

The cottage is where I was meant to stay.

The night stretches on as Keeks and I face each other - her slowly melting by choice and me fading by no fault of my own. I can no longer hold onto the last flames of myself, keeping them from touching her. And do I not owe it to myself to burn bright one last time? To go out on my own terms, rather than allowing my circumstances to suffocate me?

I do.

I release my tight grip on the firestorm that I am and burn

thoroughly. At first, Keeks blinks back shocked tears as she faces my flame. A look of understanding dawns on her features as she realizes this is my final inferno, that soon all I will become is smoke up the chimney, leaving to drift away on the winter breeze.

Finally, I might know what the world around me looks like.

She stands, stretching, attempting to shake off the slushed ice from her features. She whimpers at me, high and piercing, the most desperate sound I have ever heard her make.

I know, my friend. I don't want to live without you either.

Cold surrounds me, my fire having finally found what will be its true end. At first, it is as bitter as they say. It becomes a numbing force, a feeling I could not replicate if I desired to try.

A quiet resolve shows in the gleam of Keeks' eyes. She lingers, nearer to me than ever before. It's as if the cottage itself has held its breath, waiting to see what is to happen next. She leaves a trail of melted frost as she walks closer to me, tentatively stepping into my bed of timber and ashes.

If this is my last day, my final moment, then I will burn.

Keeks curls into me, gifting me the touch of a friend in my final moments. And at last, I know what the touch of snow feels like.

Somehow, it feels like a piece I've been missing all along.

She melts into me, surely losing her own consciousness as her life force seeps into my last ember, extinguishing me once and for all.

As we slip off into what may come next for beings like us, we are one. A familiar melody sounds as I drift away on the breeze. It reminds me of the arrival of tired footsteps - the creak of cold, worn hinges.

WHAT ONCE WAS OURS

We spend the night buried in an edge of cold - a tinge of regret. Ceraphina refuses to light a match that evening, grief burying her as I attempt to rest.

As dawn arises, we are met with a silence ringing in our ears. There is no chirp of our fox, no crackle of our fire. Being as we are, we are overly in-tune with our surroundings. Our eyes are sharper, our ears clear. We have no true need for a flame's glow, especially as the morning sun rises in the east, but it was a comfort we had come to rely on, in a way.

We had quickly become just us two, all those years ago. After… our tragedy. The presence of our gifts was a steady hum, a kind comfort that we hadn't realized we valued so much.

Only in absence do we truly see the weight of what we had.

And by then, it's far too late.

We pack our few belongings, leaving behind the cottage we know. Ceraphina and I don't speak, but our collective sadness hangs between us like a taut thread. We were not meant to part with our gifts like this. They were meant to make the journey with us, to our past land, joining with us for a new start. We had journeyed as far as we were able yesterday, farther than we should have gone, only to return and find that everything had changed within our four cottage walls.

So now, there is no reason to stay, or to take our time packing up and leaving.

Our gifts are gone.

The wind whispers through the leaves, telling us this place is no longer our home.

We know. We feel it so deeply.

Ceraphina stands at the edge of our winter garden, ready to move onto the next place, her maroon hair flowing behind the tips of her ears. The bond between us tells me her heart is heavy as mine is - that her chest is tight and unyielding.

Elynia's trees are ancient, but as we make our way down a worn, hidden path, they age. Over the years, we've traveled this way frequently, begging the bark surrounding us for a glimpse of our kind. Though we just walked this familiar ground yesterday, I still feel off-course.

My hands twitch, restless as ever, and my usual smooth gait falters. There is a hollow absence within me now. The pain of the past lingers within my heart. We were not awarded the chance to say goodbye to our kind when we went into hiding, and now, it is the same to be said for our gifts to each other.

What does this mean for the two of us? Are we doomed to the same fate?

My soul is crushed beneath the weight of longing that I have inside - the longing I feel to return to our true home. Perhaps that might fix everything that has gone wrong.

Unfamiliar earth looms in front of us.

We are lost.

Ceraphina looks back at me, questioning, from where she leads us. A leather bag made of her own hands hangs from her shoulder, carrying our few artifacts and trinkets we have kept ever since they came to destroy everything so many years prior.

The trees are not singing.

Her mind enters my head like silk. The bond that we share has intertwined our souls - our minds. There have been days I forget what my own voice sounds like, as it is not a habit to use it often.

The crunch of snow beneath our boots fills the woods. She pauses, hand brushing over the stark tip of a pine tree beside us, its colors faded and dull.

Perhaps we are too late.

WE CANNOT BE.

Her voice rings out loud within me, and my eyes widen in shock. I know what she is thinking: where is the song of the earth? The melody of the trees? If we were close to our kind, even Elynia itself would not be able to hold back it's harmonious sound.

I do not answer her - do not need to. She knows I feel the weight of our delay just as she does. And more so than that, what could I say? How could I assure her that we will find what we are looking for when I'm not sure myself? This is the very reason it has taken us so long to go back.

We have been afraid.

As we continue, this part of the forest is no longer familiar to us. In all of our travels, we've never dared to stray this far, rushing back to end the day, recapping stories of our travels to our gifts. We slowed our travels too much yesterday. Now, there is no such time restraint. We must not let it be in vain.

Silence has settled here, thick and suffocating. Before, this space would have been a chorus of life - pulsating through every leaf, petal, stream. There is not even the scurry of wildlife left, as if the earth itself mourns what we lost.

We have been gone for so long. I reach out on our bond, giving it a gentle caress. For years, it has been but her and I, and I have cherished that. Others of us were not so lucky to have a loved one beside them - there was not enough time, no warning to be given.

What if home has forgotten us?

Her thoughts are barely a whisper, as if she couldn't quite find the strength to reach me.

I lengthen my stride and reach for her hand, my palm brushing lightly against hers as our fingers intertwine. A spark passes between us, reminding me that whether we find what we are looking for or not, our presence together remains the same.

We started over once - we can do it again.

This is meant to be a comforting remark, but I know she would scoff at it. We do not completely desire to start fresh - to begin anew. We only long for what we once had.

We had gone on too long without coming back to this place - The Clyrn. Held as a secret by our own, the location was betrayed by our very heir to the rulers of Elynia. The ruler's kind came in the night - brandishing torches, arrows made of ash, and spears of iron.

It tore our world apart. Even with our magic, it was not enough. Houses burned, families were taken prisoner, and animals were killed. We barely made it out in the end, having lived on the outskirts. I had prepared for this - for war. When we built our home, I had crafted a hidden compartment in our floorboards. Barely big enough to fit us both, we waited in there for eternity.

Many times, steps had sounded above us, voices mumbling from those sent to kill. When we deemed it safe to exit, everything was cinders around us.

There was no one - and no thing - left.

Our people had fallen.

We buried the bodies we could find, taking care to prepare them for what may come next. We cast an illusion upon ourselves, changing our features to be more like those that reside in the towns within Elynia - to hide in plain sight - while we found a new place to call home.

We never traveled far from The Clyrn, always within a few days journey.

Just in case.

A ripple of pain washes over me, sharp and raw. I had not realized I was projecting my memories through our bond. I wipe them away, hoping to bring her relief. I need to be strong for her - for us.

But what is strength if not the pain that comes with change?

Steps crunch as we reach a quiet, empty expanse.

I hardly recognize what I'm looking at.

The land is barren in many places, empty stretches of grass where wildflowers used to grow thick and wild. The trees - once towering and alive - are now withered, black with soot, and broken.

My heart breaks. I had not realized just how tightly I was holding onto that thread of hope - regardless how small - that things would be better when we returned.

New.

There are no houses now. There is no lively conversation around the campfire, or songs sung beside the river. It had been a place of peace. A sanctuary for us all. We ran barefoot in the cool grass, laughing under a wide open sky. The river, once clear and sparkling, was now but a stagnant trickle. The clearing is overrun with thorny brambles, shattered glass, and broken dreams.

I had not realized it would still be this bad.

I reach out a hand, caressing her fingertips. Tears form in the corners of her eyes and it's all I can do to keep myself from wiping them. I know I must let her feel - must allow her to fully grieve so we can begin again.

I thought... I thought we might not be the first to return. We heard whispers... that we were ready to rise again.

I squeeze her hand.

We will find something. Start searching.

Ceraphina closes her eyes, just for a moment. I watch her chest rise and fall, mimicking the motion with my own. I know she's tuning into the presence of the forest around her, though not quite as much as I am able due to the nature of our abilities. The winter snow and frosted ice calls to me, asking me to lean into it. But still, nothing stirs. No creatures rustle in the underbrush, no sounds linger in the air.

It's as though our world has forgotten how to live.

My mind wanders as I touch debris, moving sleet-covered burnt remnants of what was. Brittle bark crumbles in my hands, the scent of ash taking over my senses. I think of the days long past, before flames devoured our secret place.

My memories of 'then' were once vivid and sharp, but now they are but wisps of wind flitting through my brain. The years spent surrounded by family and friends are long gone, and an eternity apart causes the color to leach from what I remember.

So carefree, so eager to learn and grow and worship our gods. I once could distinguish our people by their voices, so clear and pure, but now I'm not sure I'd recognize them if we did find a trace of their being.

It's much more complex for Ceraphina. She was the closest

thing to a sister the heir of The Clyrn had.

And it was that heir that brought on our ruin.

She is no stranger to an all-consuming flame, but I wonder if she ever thought her gift would be what brought our demise?

I fall to my knees - bitter and helpless. My hands are covered in age-old ash, the night now overcoming us swiftly and all at once. Our home no longer exists - there is nothing for us to go back to. Everything has been ravaged - scarred by the loss of our people and our gifts. Our gods have abandoned us.

What are you meant to do when the place you longed to return to is nothing like you hoped it would be?

We are scattered - lost to the wind.

With no hope of return.

We had fought so valiantly, bled so brightly, but in the end, we lost. And all that was left was this - a husk of a place that no longer recognizes us.

I catch a glimpse of Ceraphina from across the way, her eyes meeting mine. Her gaze was once full of fire and life, but is now distant and clouded with a sadness that mirrors my own. I feel her heart break in time with mine, a reminder that we are one and will be until the shadows claim us.

I stay tethered to her - the one last sliver of home that I have.

I lift myself up, brushing the debris off my knees so we may walk together, deeper into the middle of what had once been our home. Our feet brush against the uneven earth, silence broken by the soft rustling of our movement. We reach the center of The Clyrn where an ancient oak once stood - a symbol of our unity and immortality.

It was under that tree that Ceraphina and I joined together as one, and before that, where we had met for the first time.

It was the first thing they set fire to.

Once the very heart of our community, it is now but a hollow shell. Cracked and split, branches twisted into unnatural angles.

Ceraphina stands before the tree, hand trembling as she touches the charred bark.

This is not what I thought we'd find.

There is sorrow in her tone, but also a touch of resilience that I have not seen from her in years.

We must begin again.

She kneels in the hard dirt, reaching into her bag. A sapling emerges from it, her hands gentle and steady as she picks it up. Ceraphina digs into the ground, dirt filling her nails and caking her fingertips. She plants the small oak, painstakingly covering its roots.

As she places this small offering in the ground, a kernel of hope begins to take root in my chest. Perhaps this new tree can bring prosperity and renewal to The Clyrn. Together, we can make this place a better home than it was before. As long as I have Ceraphina, I have all I need.

Her face finds mine, so familiar and yet, so changed. The years have taken their toll on her, as they have on myself. We are both so different now, so far removed from the free lovers we once were.

I kneel beside her, covering the rest of the young tree together. Though winter lingers, spring is coming, and together we will find a way to make this tree grow strong.

And here, in this moment, kneeling before the ruin of our home, we are connected. And we *can* begin again. We can take back what once was ours.

And maybe, one day, that would be enough.

Maybe it always was.

FORSAKEN ROOTS

The stretch of time is a painful ache when you know it may have no end.

I have stayed steadfast here for longer than I can recall. The world around me has always been in motion, others passing through, seasons wreaking havoc, animals nesting only to depart once again. But I have remained the same - tethered to the earth, my branches stretching ever upward. The only sign of time passing is the transformational thickening of my trunk, growing stronger with age. I am a silent witness to Elynia's constant shifting, yet I myself do not change.

Birds of various colors make their homes hidden in my leaves, small rodents burrow within me to rest for the heavy winter we are under. Deer lie down within my shade when the weather is warmer, finding comfort from our brutal sun. These animals are a flurry of activity, a glimpse of the busyness ever constant within our ripening town.

I protect them from the elements, but who will protect me? Who will lay with me for warmth, or take time to chatter frequently back and forth?

They move, they change, they grow, they leave. But me? I am here to stay. My roots have forsaken me, molding me to this very spot for not just a lifetime, but for an eternity. I am always here, in the center of The Clyrn, motionless. My leaves turn from green to gold to brown and back, but I have never *truly* known change.

I stand in the middle of a clearing, meant to be a symbol of unity and rebirth. The town around me has grown since I was just a sapling, grappling for the nutrients needed to stay strong as they were. My two Caretakers nurtured me - keeping me within good health when I was a sapling. They made sure I was fed, watered, standing straight and growing readily. As I reached my peak, their attention tapered off, seeing that I was self-sufficient enough to take care of myself.

I've watched young trees on the outskirts of our town, branches bending in the wind, their leaves fluttering as if they were made to dance. I envy them, for they grow together - their twigs intertwined, their roots surely braided in conjunction with one another. They stand firm as one, keeping us safe from those looking to harm what has been built around me.

I stand alone.

Isolated.

The forest encompassing the town before me is filled with the sounds of life - chirping birds, singing voices, laughter, rustling leaves, the howl of wolves. It is a melody that once gave me life, but now it only reminds me of what I do not have.

One to share this moment with.

And I am silent. I have no voice to call out, no wings to fly, no legs to run and chase and follow those close. My roots remain deep in the ground, the gritty dirt covering my rough surface in the only embrace I've ever known.

My Caretaker's people flit around me, graceful as sunlight caught in a breeze, their laughter more vibrant with each passing day. There is a brightness to their lives - a vividness -

that took years to come into fruition.

It was not always like this.

Once, it was just me and my Caretakers. They began to build their town around me, whispering sweet words to one another as they passed, hands brushing, creating worlds of meaning in the space between them.

I had considered myself an extension of them at the time - a trio rather than a duo. But as others like them found our hidden space, as the town grew, I began to feel resentful. No longer were their stories shared beneath my branches - now it is joy shared within homes and under the stars.

I watch the town's children, their excitement like the rippling of streams, chasing each other beneath me and around me. They climb high into my height, their small fingers creating deep grooves where their touch lingers, facing retribution from those older than them. I do not mind them grappling to me - it is when I feel most alive.

I witness them grow, their lives unfolding like petals of flowers when blooming. A year to them is a day to me, time creeping by in moments and seasons. Their lives seem to stretch on for an eternity, as does mine.

Oftentimes, I ache. When the space beneath my branches seems too quiet, when their voices are a distant hum, when I am left to my own happenings. I yearn for them - hoping they will notice that I am more than a place to rest or a shelter from the rain. I want to be the reason they gather, an image of togetherness for us all.

They used to sing songs of unity to me, praising my resilience and existence from morning to night. Am I no longer a symbol of importance to them?

Am I now just... a tree?

Is this what it means to outlast? Should I stay standing while everything else seems to fall away? I do not feel sturdy with age. I feel forgotten.

Wind brushes against me, but it makes me shudder. No longer the comforting breeze I have come to wish for, now it is just a brittle reminder that there is nothing else for me. Even my own leaves betray me, abandoning my branches at the first sign of winter.

Was I planted here with a purpose? Or am I simply a seed caught in the crossfire between chance and fate?

I do not know anymore what I am reaching towards, only that it is slipping through my weary branches.

The sun begins to dip below the horizon as it does every other evening. Even in the midst of a cold winter, the air is heavy with something unknown. I wait: listening, watching. It is not like The Clyrn to be thick with quiet, but the heart of the town is covered in silence. Ice begins to crust my limbs, weighing me down with every passing sweep of precipitation.

This winter storm seems endless.

And relentless.

When dawn once again arises, everything around me is covered in inches of gleaming powder. The sky is a vast stretch of pale gray, holding no hope for the season change to come.

A whistle catches my attention, as soft as the hush of falling snow. A flurry of wings disturbs the stillness I am standing in, breathing interest back into me. Tiny talons press into my bark, cutting through the snow with ease. Feathers ruffle, a dozen small bodies shifting against me, looking for warmth in the most unlikely of places. Their brown-speckled forms tuck themselves in close, burrowing into the crooks of my branches and the hollow of my bark. The family's voices rise in soft chirps, testing the stillness around them.

They hop along my arms, crafting their new home. As the days pass, I grow warm to their presence. The small heartbeats thrum against me, reminding me of the beauty of life. I become a shield for them, protecting them from the harshest of the elements.

Somewhere along the way, as they grow, I forget the heavy burden that is my isolation.

Their presence is a rhythm I have come to welcome. They dart between my roots, leaving trails in the snow to remind me of their being. Contently, I listen to their song, the whistles and trills stretching far beyond my own reach and filling the space between them and me.

As winter deepens, they choose to stay. They weave their nest into my bark, their liveliness slipping into the spaces where loneliness had taken root within me. I no longer move through the motions of a day, a month, a year. An eternity does not seem long enough when I know their lives are but a blip in the years to come.

If the birds see me, if the animals value my existence, if even the snow itself begs to lay against my form... perhaps the town *does* see me - had always known me, in its own way.

Maybe I could be more than a silent observer of their lives. Surely I am part of their story, just as they are in mine. I am a sure thing - anchored in place and permanent. My roots are woven into the fabric of their existence, my life a testament to the love that flows through them as surely as the water that runs through my being.

Something tender awakens within me, cracking open the cold shell that I have been festering in for too long.

I have never been alone.

To be the only one of myself standing here does not result in isolation - it creates a unique opportunity to share and take from those I love.

To coexist in a way that many others cannot.

The sun sets, the stars beginning to twinkle in the sky. Night has always been the hardest for me, as they all retire into their homes and I am left to stand in the dark alone. But tonight, I feel it - a touch, as soft as a sigh. Through the years, my birds are still here. They have not left me - they call me their home.

Tonight I stand tall, reaching proud into the night sky. My branches seem to grab at the stars, my roots searching for purchase deeper into this earth we share. I am part of a whole, not a lonely piece drifting by. They are so full of life, intertwined with me on this journey we call *living*.

As I reach with my roots, I find a source of new energy calling back to me. A small, delicate flower sprout nestled near my trunk.

I am taken aback. One of the birds must have dropped a seed nearby, or perhaps the earth decided spring might come early.

As days pass, I notice it growing, pushing upward through the melting drifts of snow. A new life has begun. It might have merely been a kernel that was blown in from the heavy wind, but it has chosen to grow at my feet, in the soil I have nourished for years and years.

Everyday, it grows taller, its small leaves catching morning light and its stem firming as it finds the sun. It is a small thing, fragile, yet determined. A radiant purpose stirs within me.

The length of eternity stretches forever when you have nothing to share it with. Now, I might have the opportunity to understand who I am and what I could be and pass that along to this new life. I have been part of the beauty of this town all along, and now it can be too.

The world around me was never just about the constant motion and change of seasons. No, it was also made up of quiet moments, small things that others do not notice. The way a single leaf might drift from a branch, the soft murmur of the wind, the slow stretch of roots as they dig deeper. These times are just as alive as any other.

The small sprout begins to bloom as spring comes forward, its petals unfurling delicately. I feel the call of life coming from its stalk and I wonder if it can feel me answering back.

My birds continue to chase each other as time moves along, and I grant myself permission to be *part* of the town, not merely a passerby. I hope my flower does the same, learning from me to not take a single moment for granted. Each of us are pieces that make up a larger picture - one that would be incomplete without those around us.

I am part of something bigger than myself.

But I am also the heart of all that is around me and within me. I do not move, and I remain unchanged in many ways. But being alone does not equate to the bark shattering loneliness that I allowed myself to feel. I am part of Elynia. It calls to me, reminding me that I have found my family and my purpose. It was there all along, begging to be grasped.

I have finally reached out to take hold.

WEIGHTED WINGS

These thick branches cradle me high above the forest floor, where shadows prowl in the silence and starving eyes gleam at me in the dark. The sturdy trunk blocks the icy touch of winter, its rough bark steadfast against the brutal chill. This tree has always been *mine*, as long as I can remember. But now, the chatter of beaks around me grates against me. I do not wish to share this place any longer.

My family was raised here, having found ourselves within these dark branches by accident - or was it by the wind's fate? We might never truly know. I hoped that as time passed, my family would migrate somewhere else and never return, if only to leave me alone beneath these leaves. Instead, they continuously remind me of their presence, never quieting down long enough for me to rest in solitude.

The cold breeze carries the scent of coming rain, soft and sweet, as the cusp between winter and spring merge over Elynia. I perch on the highest branch of our oak, my talons sinking into the bark, to watch over The Clyrn and all those within it. Below, my siblings dart between the branches, wings slicing through the cool air, their songs piercing the silence that does not exist.

Though this is the only home I've ever known, though our

nest below calls to me day after day, I want to *leave*.

I often wonder, is home a fixed place? Or is it possible to begin a new one, on my own, wherever I might wish?

The thought flutters inside me, the longing for freedom trapped in my very rib cage. The gray sky seems to call to me from above, vast and achingly aware that I have never strayed from what I've always had. My wings prickle at the thought, ever restless. Still, the scent of familiarity anchors me in place.

My throat tightens. If I leave, I leave it all behind. Why is it that my family is content to sit in the mundane while I crave *newness?*

A gust of wind stirs from a place I do not recognize, ruffling my feathers and nudging me forward. The air tastes of damp soil, of distant lands - something just out of reach. I glance down at my siblings - once, twice. My chest rises, deep breaths steadying the nervous adrenaline rushing through my small body.

I *must* leave.

I must find something new to call my own.

I stretch my wings wide, catching the wind as it tugs at my feathers. It lifts me, higher and higher, past the tips of my oak. The sky is vast and endless in all directions, a sea of blue dotted with soft clouds. Below, the world begins to reach out, beckoning me to come back.

For a brief moment, I turn my head, looking back at my tree one last time. My wings falter, ever slightly. And yet, I know that my tree will not miss me. Still, I will mourn the days spent tucked under its safe canopy.

But I cannot allow myself to regret the decision to *go*.

The breeze feels different today - warmer, freer. I have never gone so far, having not cared to try.

Before today.

The thought thrills me - a fresh start. A break. Something new. Saying goodbye to the heavy branches beneath me where I spent my days perched and listening to the droning voices of my kin. Forced to participate in their songs, obligated to live the same life they all do.

Familiarity is a comfort I no longer crave.

I've wasted season after season listening to the wind, wondering what else there may be. I've never been one for migration, but now the dullness of routine pains me. The freedom others have to take the wind wherever it leads them fuels me wholly.

I'm done here.

I've heard whispers of a place beyond The Clyrn, where the waters sing with magic and glisten in the starlight. I want it. All I can grasp and hold onto and experience - I hunger for every bit of it. I will leave this life behind and start anew without the burden of the shadows of my family hanging over me and watching my every move.

I will no longer share.

I fly through the rest of the day, my wings burning with the weight of my decision and the effort I strain to give, but I do not stop. I don't need to. I don't *want* to.

I pass through the familiar first - flashes of trees I've known my whole life, rivers I've bathed in, rocky outcroppings where we might perch to sunbathe when the weather allows it. I do not look down. It's too easy to imagine myself turning back, forgetting this adventure and journey I've committed myself to and fall back into the rhythm of my old life.

But I've outgrown that life.

The very life that pulls at me now - a relentless tug deep inside of me. Maybe it's the love of my tree, or the memories

I've hidden away. Perhaps it's that the sky feels different now that I'm leaving.

I will not say goodbye.

I will not feel regret.

I will not sit in my doubt.

I will do what I know best - fly.

There's a fog in the air now, the sun hidden behind thick clouds. The wind has picked up, rocking me off course, carrying a chill that I feel to my bones. I feel as though I'm being watched, a whisper of darkness soft and insistent nestled within me.

I soar higher to escape the burden of the mist but it continually closes in on me. The landscape below is blurry, the ground nonexistent.

Was this a mistake?

I hesitate, for a moment.

The wind carries on it the ghost of the voices of my brothers, calling for me to return.

A memory of warmth, of soft feathers nestled next to me surfaces within my mind.

I shake my head, ridding the thought from my brain.

The fog doesn't lift, the air heavy. I don't know how long I've been flying and I'm not sure where I am anymore. I feel it then - the fear that comes from knowing I made a choice and must live with it, that there is no immediate way back.

I do not know the way.

The sky above me is no longer endless, but a dark, gray void as night swallows me whole. I haven't seen anything familiar in… days? Time is fleeting. It's possible I am not headed in the right direction and that I never was. I don't remember the last time I felt the warmth of the sun.

Why did I give into this desire?

Why must my restless soul crave change?

Why was I given *wings* if not to *use them*?

My short wings stop for a moment, letting the wind catch me and slow my descent. I am tired. My muscles ache. My thoughts are a blur of indecision, but then I hear something.

The faintest rustling of leaves, carried by the breeze.

And a song.

It's soft, but surely familiar. The gentle chirp of an elder, the same song my brothers and I sang together. A rasp of our call as dawn arises, calming the rest of us when the morning became too quiet. A reminder that we all made it through the night, that we were together and *okay.*

My heart lurches, briefly longing for the comfort of what I've left behind.

My body is heavy with the weight of my own thoughts, and I wonder, have I not flown far enough already to experience the newness I crave?

Perhaps below will be the land that called to me - a land of tall trees, magic rivers, and a new home.

I must check.

The gray mist dissipates as I descend, the horizon fading in order to allow space in my mind's eye for what is looming right in front of me.

The sun begins to rise as dawn intrudes, its reflection in my eyes.

I stop for a moment, perched on a rock high above the earth on a cliff, and begin to hop along the ground in search of measly crumbs to fuel me for whatever the day may have for me. The song still rings in my head, calling to me, asking me to join in.

My feathers are ruffled, my short tail tired from being flicked by the wind.

I feel the exhaustion deep in my bones.

The wind begins to die down as the sun begins its ascent into the bright sky. The clouds have parted, revealing the faint outline of hills in the distance. So different is the air now than it was yesterday.

Perhaps it's a sign.

Desperation rises within me so quickly I can hardly breathe. The slight trickle of water catches my attention, thirst gnawing at me on the inside. A stream drizzles down below and I make my way, hopping all the way to give my wings a much deserved break.

I rest at the river, but do not let my guard down. My stout bill fills with water, and I tip my head back to let the liquid rush down my throat and quench my thirst. Back and forth I drink, keeping my eyes alert. After drinking my fill, movement catches my eye at a small pool of water not far from me, underneath a bit of cool shade.

A being resides there, one that I had only heard our Gatherers speak of in stories. I had not understood the magic of what they truly meant until this moment.

A *nymph*.

Lying on a bed of grass, she has one hand lightly in the water, rippling the surface as she gazes at herself. Her locks shimmer with the hues of the river at dawn - light, bright. Her movements as she rests are fluid and graceful like the current itself, her presence blending effortlessly with the mist of the riverbank to the point where I am unable to see where she ends and the stream begins.

Her skin seems to glow of moonlight, her eyes aware and as blue as the brightest of rivers. There is a quiet power in her, one that speaks to me.

For a moment, she glances up, seeming to recognize my presence. Her finger continues to draw circles in the water's surface, her hair drifting on the breeze. She tilts her head at me, and I reciprocate the gesture. As she looks at me, I feel a thread between the two of us - nature connecting our kinds through it's own ways.

You will find what you're looking for.

Her voice is like a summer rain within my mind, caressing my feathers in a warm embrace.

She resumes to what she was doing, peering at her reflection in the water's waves, leaving me to wonder where I should go next. Our broken eye contact severs the thread of connection I felt a moment ago, leaving me searching once again.

Will I find what I'm looking for? My weary, weighted wings have lost all hope.

I take off once more, gliding on a wind that is different from what I felt yesterday. It's softer, kinder, offering me reprieve from the ache in my bones. The sky is clearer, as though the clouds are parting just for me - showing me the way.

A renewed sense of determination hits me, shaking me to my core.

I fly lower, and the landscape begins to take shape - the rivers glistening, the forest taller than trees I've ever set eyes on, the rise of hills and dips of valleys abound before me.

I land softly on a flimsy branch, my heart racing as I look around. This grove is buzzing - alive with activity. Birds who look just like me and birds who don't, hopping around and singing a vibrant song - one that doesn't immediately aggravate me. The scent of leaves and earth hit me, and the sounds here are both familiar and new all at once.

I feel as though the world is holding its breath, waiting for me to jump in with both feet first.

My hesitation is interrupted by a flutter of wings, brown, white and black colors coming into view before me, blending into the shadows of the leaves.

I hesitate, watching them hop around, pecking at the bark. Our eyes meet as they look up.

Their gaze flickers with something I can't read.

Perhaps, delight? Excitement? A love for the life that they live?

Oh how I long to relate.

Maybe they could show me how.

A chill runs down my spine, but I try to mask it.

Is this the place I was searching for?

Slowly, I shift my focus to that of the young tree I reside on. Its branches stretch to the sky, reminding me of *my* tree. But maybe I could build a new home, here, with this tree.

One to call my own.

My sense of home is not slipping away, no. It's only just arriving within me, swelling my chest, beckoning me to sing a new song.

The sun climbs to the center of the sky, basking us in its rays. The bird next to me flutters its wings, as if shaking off stress of the night before. It chirps at me, but I stay silent. Giving up, it flees, joining a group for a stretch of flight.

I spend the next few days perched in this new tree, watching life go on without me, not straying far enough to truly explore.

Yet.

I want to call out, to join their song with my own, but I feel so small. I am but an intruder in a place that they claimed first.

The bird comes by to visit sometimes, placing offerings on my branch, assessing me quickly and moving on. The silence between us weighs down on me, reminding me of everything I left behind.

My kind are rarely alone, yet I have been the one to place myself in this isolation.

It's early in the morning when I hear it. I have been avoiding it, their songs at dawn, but today it pulls at me like a string. Persistently, it leads me deeper into the forest, towards a glade teeming with birds of all sorts, all colors.

I fly in, looking for a place to land and hide - to observe what is happening. There is no such place. The glade is wide open, no shadows to be seen to blend into, as if that was by no accident.

I choose to land, a moment of confidence and the lack of other options inspiring me to not hide. For if I were to turn back, who's to say how long it might be before I make the trip back home? That is not an embarrassment I'm willing to live through.

I land in the middle of bustling activity, the wind gently caressing my feathers, as if encouraging me forward. For the first time since I left The Clyrn, I feel peace.

The glade is suddenly quiet, everyone noticing me. A stranger within my own feathers, now a stranger to those around me.

There's something in their eyes - assessing me.

The bird who found me first comes forward, landing next to me. They chirp that same song - the one I remember and know like my own heartbeat. They tilt their head, asking a silent question.

Before I've made up my own mind on whether or not to engage, I chirp back.

Taken aback, excitement lights in its eyes. It chirps again, the next part of the melody.

I complete the song.

The other birds begin to land, a vibrancy of *life* weaving a tapestry before my eyes. Music bursts from their beaks, excitingly joining in to the song of my family.

Of my kin.

Of *home*.

I will carry my tree with me, tucked deep in my heart. I'll carry their song and shout it as loudly as I am able. And should I ever need to return to that place from where I came, I know the way. It will always be there, waiting for me.

But for now, the sky is wide and the rest of Elynia is waiting.

And I am ready.

I glide on the wind with others around me, the cool rush of air beneath my wings. Everything stretches out before me, infinite and full. There's a thrill within me as I dip and dive, learning the curves and spaces of my new home.

The weight of my wings has been lifted.

I am free.

MY RIVER'S EMBRACE

My river curls through the emerald forest like a silver ribbon, its surface shimmering with a thousand recognizable hues . I briefly release its tight grip on me to lay beside it, one finger trailing through the ripples like a cloud moving through the atmosphere above.

How I wish I could be up there instead.

A sparrow comes to sit and drink at my river, stealing my attention. Such a pretty, lucky thing. Wings meant to take it anywhere it desires. My restless soul screams at me to fly - to glide. I crave the warmth of the sun on my back, the pull of the wind asking me to follow or fight. The opportunity to be anywhere but trapped here under the pull of the current.

I watch it quench its thirst, its movements quick and purposeful. I look away, bitter with jealousy. Everyday I lie here, watching the world and its creatures go by. Free to choose where they will go and what they will do, just as this sparrow does.

I feel its eyes on me not a minute later, and I glance up, our gazes connecting for one moment in time. I continue to lazily swirl my finger in the waters, reminding myself of the cage I am placed in. I tilt my head, taking in the small bird as it takes me in.

You will find what you're looking for, I think, my thoughts toward the bird coated in envy. I wish profusely that I might have what it does. Guiltily, I look back down at my reflection, not wanting to think such thoughts against another of nature's kind. It is not the sparrow's fault that fate shaped me from water and not from air.

A flutter of wings whistles on the wind towards me, the breeze creating a draft on my face. My chest tightens with a sharp pang as I look up, only to find that the bird has departed where it stood.

Left behind, as always.

This is not who I was made to be.

Why would I have this desire to leave and yet be tethered to my river? Surely fairness looks at me and laughs.

The earth joins in, as my sisters do.

I am bound here. My world is beautiful, yes, but it is small. Constantly hemmed in by trees and stone that I cannot fully leave to explore. I gaze at the stream before me, my pale, glowing form reflected back at me. My hair flows like currents over my shoulders, my skin translucent and glistening as though kissed by the dew surrounding me on an early morning.

I frown at myself, wholly unimpressed.

My image wavers, shifting with the ripples. My eyes, large and alert, do not seem to belong to me. My lips as if borrowed from someone else. My face, round and youthful, feels like a mask - a lie whispered to me by the river I call home.

I dig my fingers deeper with force into the waters and the reflection shatters, fragments rippling outward until they disappear.

Why does the water's reflection reveal a stranger within my skin?

When will it show a picture of who I *truly* am?

My heart aches with a longing so deep it has no name. I am the river - I *know* this. The currents course through my veins, the reeds sing my songs, the moonlight paints images of my dreams across the waters. Yet I feel apart from it, as though I am just a shadow cast upon its surface.

The forest around me grows darker as the day wanes, the sun sinking behind the canopy. I rise, my movements graceful yet hesitant, and I slip into the gentle current. Because of the river's hold on me, I am only able to wander as far as I'm able to touch liquid stream.

My bare feet whisper against slippery moss and stone as I follow my river upstream, drawn by a restlessness within me that I cannot deny any longer.

I come to a small clearing where my river divides, the water parting like my hair in the current. One stream rushes forward, wild and untamed - alive with power and eager to *move*. The other is a silent hum, quiet and calm, as though reluctant to leave. The contrast settles something in me, a quiet recognition that I, too, can be contradicting.

I stand in the in-between, my toes curling against cool stone, and close my eyes. The roar of the waters drown out the constant nagging in my mind and for a moment, I feel peace.

I begin to watch the currents weave on each side of the river bend, avoiding scattered stones and fallen branches - obstacles in their way, but rather than resisting them, they embrace. And in that moment, as the wind stirs branches overhead and the water hums at me, I feel truly understood.

But still, the longing remains. I kneel at the edge of the split and dip my hands into the rushing waves, letting the icy flow course through my fingers. My river carries stories of distant lands and hidden depths beneath them, tales of transformation and rebirth - things that I will never get to experience myself.

But, perhaps I could?

I listen to the roar of it all, my heart quickening as I feel the pulse of something greater, something endless and ever-changing calling out to me. For so long I have believed that my river is incapable of change - that it is and always will be the same waters flowing through and around me. But that is far from the truth.

The rivers are always changing their shape, flowing and carving through the land with determination I wish to steal.

I never step into the same river twice. The cold liquid that swirls around me now is not the same that touched me just a moment before. The current has moved on, quickly passing me by, slipping from my tight grasp before I can fully hold onto it.

I wander through these unknown waters, leaving the separation behind. I move carefully, my steps deliberate as I trace the path of the raging stream. I feel myself unraveling, my old self slipping away like mist to match its mood.

I reach a place where the river spills into a vast waterfall, the currents plummeting to the lake beneath. The spray from the sparkling drop hits me even at this height, coating my body with a light caress.

The lake spreads wide, the edges unknown and unseen from where I stand. Perhaps it goes on and on forever, or maybe it ends just past where my eyesight is able to reach. Still, it breathes life into me, reminding me that *our courses are not fixed.*

My river twists and turns, splits and rejoins, and other times might vanish entirely just to emerge stronger somewhere else in Elynia or the lands beyond. In my mind's eye, I visualize high cliffs where my river's source springs forth, and deep dives where it descends into hidden valleys tucked beneath stone.

Each new place reveals a fragment of my very essence, showing me that if I choose, I could scatter like droplets of precipitation across this world.

Cold and sudden, a single drop of rain falls, coating my shoulder. I look up, startled, my heart swelling with pleasure as the sky darkens and the heavens open. The rain comes then in a torrent, each drop a prism that dances across my body, inviting me to take part in the freedom is has offered me.

I lift my face to the storm, letting the rain wash over me. It soaks my very being, my *complete* soul, until I feel as though I am *one* with it.

I dissolve into the sky, the earth, and the river under me. Now, I am not just my river, bound to its banks and currents. I am *every* river - whichever piece of it I might choose. I am the water itself, unable to be contained and wholly my own. I could be a gentle stream or a raging sea. I can flow, crash, rise, fall, and rise again.

A laugh escapes my lips as the rain mingles with my tears, my heart letting go of the reflection I had once clung to so tightly, my arms now stretched wide and inviting. I am new, unshackled and *me*.

I run back to my river bend, taking the long way this time, through the reeds and tall grass, up the hills and down, the storm allowing me a brief moment in time to separate from the waters that I've known all my life.

Still, I must return. I miss my river's gentle warmth, the soft ripples I play with in the shadows. I can hear it calling to me, inviting me to slip back into its kindness.

I step back into my river's embrace, my form melting into the currents as I allow myself to be carried away. The water bears me gently, cradling me as I reform to be part of everything and nothing all at once.

A mindless numbing comes over me and I do not look back, contentment flooding my bones as I flow forward and onward. I do not fear the next wave that might sweep me away, for I know my river has me.

And together, we are a ceaseless tide.

LOST FRAGMENTS

I awaken with a roar, shaking the heavens as I come into being. My presence spreads wide, coiling through the sky like a wave hitting the shore. I am vast, unknowable, powerful, new. As I crackle into existence, I know nothing, remembering only lost fragments of the last moment I began and ended. My thoughts are fleeting, scattered like the drops of rain that are beginning to fall.

Who am I?
Where am I?

The questions within me dissolve as quickly as they appear, swept away by the winds that make up my form.

Below me, this land awaits. This one is called Elynia - somehow I know this. Perhaps I have been here before. Still, land is land. In the end, they all have need for my intensity and flood. I hear them calling out to me - asking me to set them free.

I will. I must.

The patchwork of landscape sprawls beneath as I unravel, its forests whispering ancient secrets, begging me to listen. Rivers wind like veins through the flesh of the earth. I am connected to this world, stuck in an endless cycle, but I am not the land. No, I am above it - untouchable, unbound. My dark clouds churn with purpose, yet it is a purpose I do not remember choosing. Perhaps I never did. I must only be a fleeting thought of the universe, meant to rage and then be forgotten.

I expand further, the edges of my consciousness swirling out to touch the land far below me. The mountains pierce the sky, the forests beckon me closer, and the jagged edges of the rest of Elynia are etched with the passage of time that I will never fully comprehend. My winds sweep over cliffs and I am met with silence. It is not they who will remember me. No, they are a fixed entity. Only after centuries of pushing am I able to make changes to them.

I long to go further, find something, someone - anyone - to witness my existence and stand in *awe*.

I deserve that, after all. I'm the one who gives life to this world.

A vast plain lies ahead, scattered with rocks and ancient stones that protrude from the earth in an attempt to taunt me. Among them, a single boulder draws my attention. It looms, weathered, scarred with countless cracks, as if it has stood through endless cycles of creation and destruction. I descend, my winds curling around it, probing its surface with curiosity.

How is it that a single being might lay untouched through so much transformation?

That's about to change.

The rock lies silent, unyielding to my call. Should I stay for days, months, years, it might. But I never stick around that long. There is something within it here, a protectiveness that beckons to me. Fury floods my clouds at its audacity to be unrelenting.

I lash out, ruthless, my lightning splitting the air as I strike the stone. The earth trembles at the impact, yet the boulder remains, unmoved and unbroken. Frustration surges through me, a tempest of rage and longing. Why does it refuse to respond?

How dare it not acknowledge me.

My rage is not to be met with silence.

I circle once again, my rains cascading over its surface, pooling in its cracks and crevices. The water flows heavily downward, tracing ancient paths carved only by time and erosion. In these patterns, I see a reflection of myself, slowly changing yet still bound to the same cycles.

The boulder must have endured me before, I realize. It has weathered storms like me for centuries, perhaps millennia. It has withstood certain fury and remained intact. The thought strikes me, though I do not know fully why. Perhaps it is because time is not a liberty I am able to take advantage of. I must come to terms with the pieces I remember as quickly as possible, and not dwell on what could be different.

I slow, taken aback, my winds softening to a whisper as I gather around the stone. I attempt to be gentle, this time. The storm within me quiets and possibly for the first time ever, I feel something strange - a yearning to understand and connect. The rock cannot speak, nor move, yet it exists in solitude and with contentment to just *be*.

It witnesses and participates in the world in a steadfast manner. I wonder what it would say to me if it could - what secrets it holds within its hardy form.

Time stretches and I linger, crackling with energy that makes me restless. I have not felt this powerful since...

When?

I cannot recall, though I know for certain that this is something I've felt before. It's undeniable, familiar, unrelenting. How frustrating it is to be a mere passerby in your own life, one that is unable to truly and fully participate in all that you desire.

My rains continue to fall on their own, soaking the ground

around the rock until its once-dry soil turns to mud. The rock is covered now, the mud pulling it under. As my storm continues, I wander internally, my consciousness lulling me. Until suddenly, something small hesitantly stirs out of the sloppy earth. A being I mistook for the simple stone - a turtle.

I cannot recall the last time I saw such a creature, though that is no surprise to me. Its shell is rough and etched with patterns I saw before as it moves, my blunt fury wrestling it out of a supposed slumber. It emerges, finally, its movements slow and purposeful.

Perhaps it is bothered by my presence. This might be the moment I am acknowledged.

Still, I cannot yield.

As much as I can, I watch, intrigued by the creature's deliberate pace. It carries its world upon its back, an existence so different from my own vast and incomprehensible form. My wind curls around it, gentle, as I move with it. It pauses at the edge of a shallow pool my shower has created, its eyes reflecting the dim light of my clouds.

For a moment, I imagine it looking at me, something *truly* seeing me. I pull back, startled at the thought, unsure of what to make of this fragile life.

Its journey is unhurried and I feel a wrestling within me. I am anything but slow. I do not know how to be anything but what I am.

I am the crash of waves, the torrent of rain, the flash of light, the gust of wind. The turtle rests easily, as though always able to find refuge from the world above it.

Refuge from me.

My rain washes over the turtle, a soft rhythm that contrasts with the chaos I usually bring. In this moment, I try to not be a destroyer. I pull back.

I am a witness.

As I watch, a thread pulls me toward the animal. We are connected: the turtle and the storm. The turtle is intentional, a testament to patience and resilience. I am fleeting, a burst of energy that continually comes and goes, leaving hardly a lasting mark by the day. Together, we are simply a rhythm of life.

I wonder what it thinks. What it wants from its journey. What it *craves*.

Does it feel the weight of the world it carries within itself? Does it find peace within its own self-contained universe? The turtle tilts its head upward, as if relishing my rains. Its face is illuminated by the flicker of my lightning and it does not seem to fear me. It does not flee. It simply *stays.*

What would my life be like if I were allowed the chance to stay?

I will never know. That is not what I have been given.

I've made my peace with it, though that contentment is always temporary.

Time slips away as I do. I cling onto this moment, trying to linger in it as long as I am able. My storm begins to weaken, my winds dying to a whisper and my rains falling in a gentle mist. I am unraveling once again, my edges fraying as I pour out the rest of myself. The world around grows still, the anchor of my wrath slipping from my grasp.

The sky lightens, the first hints of dawn breaking through my dissipating clouds. Something hums beneath my light touch, resonating with a frequency I cannot hear but one I feel through the end of myself. It is not a sound, but a memory on the edge of my consciousness.

I've been here before.
Maybe I like it here.

It passes by me in a whisper, not faring to stay long. In the end, it doesn't matter how much I enjoy where I start. My ending is a piece of something larger - something I continually lose and can never reach. I am a necessary being to those around me, but I am not in control of when I stay and when I go.

The moment fades, frustration rising within me but I am unable to do anything of substance with it. This is the end, not the beginning. The storm within me stirs, restless and yearning, as I rise and begin to drift away. The land below is more distant, everything within it shrinking to specks among the vastness of Elynia and the worlds beyond.

I wonder if the turtle might remember me after this - might carry some trace of my presence with it during its journey. But even as I wonder, the memory of the moments we had together begins to fade, slipping through my grasp like the water through my clouds.

I drift higher, a sense of melancholy washing over me. The world feels indifferent, and I am but a fleeting minute within it. I hold onto the connection I briefly felt with the earth, the short harmony that hit me. My essence begins to scatter like lightning, and I am unraveling, becoming nothing and everything all at once.

Before I vanish completely, I sense the faint stirrings of a new storm, far in the distance. It is like me, yet not me - a continuation of a cycle I barely understand. Perhaps I will find the turtle in another world, another life. Though if I did, I would not know it. Perhaps it will feel the same yearning, fleeting connection that I do in the way that we are all connected. I don't know, and I never will. The thought brings me a strange kind of comfort, but it is one I can't take with me where I am going.

And then, my last drop of rain suspends itself in the air, laying on its final resting place in the drenched soil.

And I am gone.

I awaken with a roar, shaking the heavens as I come into being. My presence spreads wide, coiling through the sky like a wave hitting the shore. I am vast, unknowable, powerful, new. As I crackle into existence, I know nothing, remembering only lost fragments of the last moment I began and ended. My thoughts are fleeting, scattered like the drops of rain that are beginning to fall.

Who am I?

Where am I?

The questions within me dissolve as quickly as they appear, swept away by the winds that make up my form.

Below me, this land

TANGLED PATH

To my dismay, the storm hit without warning, as it always does. One moment, the forest was still, the air thick with the smell of damp earth and a quiet hum of the wind. The next, the heavens open wide with a crackle of lightning, illuminating the trees in a sharp, blinding flash. Rain begins to fall soon after. First, as a drizzle, a mere misting upon my shell. Second, a downpour that whips the leaves overhead so quickly I can hardly stand my ground.

Ruining the peace I held, once again.

I huddle in my shell, frustrated, but comfortable. I draw my legs in close, pressing myself deep into the soaked mud. The thunder rumbles, low and heavy, as if the storm itself is groaning. The wind howls through branches and surely twists the trees, bending them and reshaping the forest I've known my whole life. Perhaps the storm is just doing its part within this cycle we are all connected by, or maybe it is searching for something that it lost.

Either way, I do not care.

This is *my* forest. I do not have time for this interruption.

While I might be a steady creature, do not mistake my slowness for patience.

I close my eyes, pulling deeper into my armor. At least that is one thing I can count on to stay the same - my shell. Though the exterior is tough and weathered, I still feel the relentless pounding of the rain on my back. Vibrations of the storm's fury shake the earth beneath me, digging me deeper into my spot. Though I am used to the rumble, I grow weary of the sudden change. My rhythm, my routine... *gone.*

All because of this *torrent.*

I feel something quick and hot hit my shell, shocking me from the inside out. It pulls me from my frustration, anger now rising swift within me. Still, I remain where I am, assessing the potential damage from where I hide within myself.

I'm not afraid. Simply... cautious.

Rain floods the surface, burying me even deeper into the mud than I was before. But then, it pulls back, seemingly gentle. Perhaps the storm is fizzling out?

I can feel it still above me, as if purposefully breathing down my neck. Why does it not relent? When will it move on?

Why must it torment me when I have done *nothing* to it?

How long will I have to wait for my life and forest to go back to normal?

Enough is enough. If it cannot respect my unspoken desires, I will move on and find a space that will.

I crawl out of my shell, deliberately sledging through the deep mud I've been buried under. The storm's wind moves as I do, tightening its hold on me that I so desperately wish to shake off. I pause at a shallow pool of water, leaves fluttering in the ripples, catching a reflection of the storm at my back.

Leave. Me. Alone.

As if it has heard my very thoughts, the thunderstorm pulls back, leaving me be. I continue on, taking my time, as it is the only way I know how to move. As the rain continues, I tilt my head upwards, hoping to wash the mud weighing me down from my back. As I move my eyesight back toward the horizon, I realize I do not recognize where I am.

I pause, giving into the confusion.

What did that storm do to my forest?

My world has changed.

Weary, I look around to survey my options as the storm *finally* moves on completely. Trees once tall and proud now lay on the ground, broken and exposed. The path I knew by heart, the one I've walked for years, has vanished beneath a flood of twisted vines and shattered wood. The scent of pine and earth has been replaced with the wet, musky scent of change.

Change I did not ask for.

I take a slow, cautious step forward, twigs breaking roughly beneath my small feet. I have never minded my pace, as it is my hesitancy that often saves my life. I am the only thing I can count on, these days. Still, it is as if the world around me is testing me, waiting to see if I will push through or if I will give up.

Perhaps I should. After all, it has always been safe within the bounds of my shell.

I do not require much. So why does Elynia taunt me so?

Everything outside of me is an outlier I have no control over. A tremor of frustration rises within me. Why does this world not respect the space I have carved for myself? Why must everything shift and change when I have made it clear that all I want is stability?

I glare at the fallen trees, feeling as though they have decided to betray me personally. I nudge at the branches with my foot, daring them to move back to where they belong.

They do not.

My surroundings never ask if I am interested in their shift - they just do. It does not ask if I am comfortable before twisting into something I do not recognize. It does not ask my permission - instead, deciding to leave me behind, causing me to scramble to make sense of the tangled path left for me.

Why does my patience, my constant stillness, not ensure the world around me moves the same way? It never listens to me. No matter how much I keep my shell firm, Elynia still grows and changes.

The world will never relent to me.

The more I fight the change happening around me, the more I am disappointed by what I see. What choice to I have but to remain in the tight confines of my shell for the rest of time?

I cannot do this anymore.

A figure suddenly steps out of the roughage before me, small and unsteady on its feet. Most beings like these stay within their own version of their shell, careful not to venture too far within Elynia. This one has come a far way to wind up here.

Especially now, after that dreadful storm.

She is fragile, young. I make myself smaller, careful not to draw her attention. She leans against a broken stump, her clothes soaked with rain and mud. Her short hair is matted, eyes dark and wild.

Just another unexpected thing in my forest that I did not ask for.

Somehow, she finds me. Her wide eyes meet mine, overly aware of her surroundings.

The forest does not make a sound as it notices her presence.

Curiosity gets the better of me, something pulling at me to get closer to her.

The girl kneels down in front of my eyes, her fingers brushing the damp earth. She breathes in deeply, sighing, eyes closed and focused. She traces the dirt, as if searching for something.

Vibrations echo from her fingertips, rippling the ground beneath me and the trees still standing above. I curl into my shell, afraid, ready to hide.

Still, I peek, for some reason unable to help myself.

Her hand continues to move, as if tethered. Trees, bushes, and grasses surrounding us pulse, their energies calling out to each other.

I shudder.

No. More. Change!

I cannot take this much longer.

A thick bundle of roots tangled in front of the girl begin to part, creating space where there wasn't any. Fallen trees magically move out of the way, branches mystically make room. The forest itself - alive, active - makes a way for her.

The path lying before me is no longer covered in debris - tangled, impassable. No, a clearing has appeared as if by the girl's will alone.

Rather than marvel at this happening, I cannot help but hold onto my bitter thoughts.

Why does the forest listen to her, but not to me? I've been here longer.

She stands, brushing off her knees, and I take a tentative step toward her. Unsure of what I've just witnessed, I wonder, could this path be for me too?

Perhaps she is just a means to an end for something that was really meant for me.

I hesitate, as I always do.

The girl looks back at me then, something in her gaze resolved. A knowing look, as if she, too, has fought against the tides of change and lost. And yet, she is here, embracing it.

I am left behind to watch as she moves ahead, picking up speed as she leaves my line of sight down the path. She certainly breathes easier, her shoulders not quite so rigid. I can feel it deep in my bones - the energy that she gives back to the forest just by standing within it.

She disappears from my eyes, and cannot bring myself to follow just yet. She moves with a purpose, as I often do. Perhaps the whispers I've heard of The Clyrn speak to her too - maybe she will find whatever she might be searching for.

I step forward, my feet more sure, attempting to trust this path that appeared before my eyes for something that was not me. It does not feel hostile, like a threat. It stretches before me, bathed in a soft light of breaking clouds, inviting me to take part in this gift.

With every step I take, my soul feels lighter. The weight of the storm and of change lift from me, and I realize just how long I've spent fighting this place. My desire for consistency, for control, has drained me.

Perhaps Elynia and I can coexist.

It is possible that the forest never meant to trap me, to lock me up. The storm abruptly happened to it, too. Maybe I was given this day as an opportunity to fight for what I truly need.

This path will show me the way, just as the forest does.

But I have to trust it, as I do myself.

As I trust my shell, my home.

I walk through trees and clearings, broken pieces the storm left behind to my right and my left. I keep a steady pace, as I always do. The sun's rays touch the earth, soaking my shell in warmth and comfort.

This forest is not a prison.

The path is my way forward.

UNWOVEN CHAINS

I run, my bare feet pounding against the cold ground like the thunder that rolled across Elynia's sky hours ago. I am bruised by both roots and stone, but I don't stop and I *won't*. The forest is dark and endless, my body just as lost as my mind.

What do I hope to find? I'm not sure anymore. I just know that the house I am leaving behind is not as kind as the refuge of trees surrounding me. I tell myself this, over and over, my chest tight with fear, my breaths short and shaky.

I have been running for hours, maybe days. Time has no meaning to me anymore. The sun has set and risen and set once again, too many times to count. My body aches, begging me for reprieve against this hard terrain, but I cannot give in to the desperation I feel.

I still sense the echoes of that house - the chilly stone floors, the walls that pressed in too close, the voices constantly raised with anger. They always demanded obedience, silence, *sacrifice*. I tried to become a mere shadow, unseen and unheard, but they always found me. My magic, they harped, was useless and a curse.

A disgrace to our kind.

My mind reminds me of the weight of their gazes, sharp and judgmental, stripping me down to nothing more than a burden.

Their barbed and bitter words still cling to my skin like scars that refuse to fade. Every mistake made - whether true or not - was met with punishments of their choosing. Every show of defiance with tightened fists, withering stares.

I made myself small, unnoticeable, doing my best to disappear before their keen eyes. Even then, it was as if the walls had ears of their own. I was never truly alone. Their control was a chain wrapped tightly around my wrists, their disappointment a tangible scent in the air.

My magic, my connection with Elynia and nature itself, was the only thing that kept me from turning into a hollow shell. It kept me alive.

Refusing to be bound forever, their chains shackling me from the inside out, I decided to run. I could no longer handle their bitterness and regret seeping into the edges of *my* life. Broken beyond belief, I tore away from that place. My roots broke away from their hardened soil. Even though the world surrounding me was unknown, it was *mine*.

The wind sings through the trees, their branches swaying and whispering to me. Both myself and the forest wrecked from the storm, I make my way through their torn bones, easing their hurt with my heart. I hear them talking about me, rustling my secrets between their dying leaves. My magic hums low in my body, warm yet tired, as if trying to maintain wakefulness.

I should call the vines, ask the roots to cover my tracks, but something small within me knows no one is following.

They do not care to find me.

I am so tired.

Perhaps the forest will protect me regardless.

Damp leaves cling to my skin, and the air I'm breathing is thick with the scent of rain. The distant call of some animal echoes, its voice a reflection of the ache within my own chest - hollow and alone.

I arrive at a small clearing before what looks like the worst of the storm's damage. My breath shudders, a small reprieve giving me a moment to think and recollect my thoughts. I stumble over a root, catching myself to lean on a broken stump, wiping my sticky hair from my eyes.

I survey my surroundings, hyper aware of what is around me, and find a turtle looking at me with curious eyes.

It peeks from the edges of its shell, dark and ridged like the old bark we are encircled with. Its tiny eyes blink slow and unbothered, but still, I sense it holds a tension that I might understand. It does not run, choosing instead to partially hide itself from me. It waits, as if wondering what I might do next.

Perhaps I'm trespassing on its territory.

I sigh. No space will ever be truly mine.

Jealousy pangs within me toward the animal, that it carries its home on its back. Always safe, always certain. It is its own protection, in a way. It holds a sure thing that others could not possibly imagine having in the first place.

The turtle blinks at me, its small body steady against the wreckage of the storm. It seems to be in no hurry - no rush to flee, like I am. Maybe it knows what I do not - that home is something you carry, not something you chase.

Still, the earth itself hurries me, as if warning me that something might be coming. Should it be *them,* I will not chance being found. The path before me is mangled with misuse, but I know I can find a way.

The forest falls silent.

Kneeling, I press my hands to the wet ground, feeling the soil beneath my fingertips connect with the blood rushing through my veins. I breathe in, deeply, eyes closed and ready. The earth is alive, vibrating with energy beneath me, and it *remembers*. I know it will know me.

I do not fear my magic, nor do I struggle with control. How could I, when the earth has been the only thing in my life that I can remember being kind to me? It continuously gives to me, and I give back.

As I trace the earth, creating patterns and rhythms that only I understand, the trees begin to right themselves. The bushes move to create a new path. The limbs and leaves and broken pieces mend themselves and become whole.

How I long to do the same.

I take a long breath, pushing myself up. I still sense the turtle near me, as if following me for a moment or two. Still, it surely remains unhurried and unafraid.

I cannot say the same about me.

But, maybe, if I cannot carry my own home, I can find one for myself.

I look back, catching a quick glance at the turtle again.

Nothing about this journey has been easy. I have searched for shelter night after night, hiding out in hollow logs, curling up beneath broad leaves when rains were relentless. I follow rivers and paths as hunger gnaws at me like the beasts I'm trying to avoid. I speak to the trees, retelling to them stories of my trials and troubles, letting them into the secret place that is my heart and mind.

I focus on my surroundings, watching for where this land might want to take me. The forest hasn't turned me away yet, choosing to not forsake me. It leads me forward and guides me.

My feet move of their own accord, leaving the clearing behind to follow the path the forest has gifted me. I pick up speed, shoulders loosening, ready for where I might go next.

Seeing nothing new for miles, I grow relentless and uneasy. Is this what my life has come to? Is this what I have put upon myself in my leaving? If the world had eyes, I know what it would see. Dirt caked upon my skin, a wild desperation in my eyes. It might *fear* me if it knew, truly, just how far I would go to escape what I was given.

I stumble upon a town, hidden in the middle of a forest that has called out to me, beckoning me to take a chance on the land here.

Whispers of something called The Clyrn... That I will be safe there.

I do not believe it, but I have no other choice.

I can always leave again, if I must.

My legs ache, my eyelids heavy. The trees clear, giving way to a little wooden cottage with a stone roof. Lanterns glow in the window, casting shadows upon the dirt. The air smells warm and inviting, like fresh herbs and something sweet. I hear the earth nudge me forward, as if truly leading me *here.* I know deep within me that the forest would not lead me astray, but still, fear overcomes my limbs.

I freeze, hesitating on the edge of the break in the woods. My heartbeat is pounding in my eyes, causing panic to seep into my bones. If I am rejected, if they return me to my captors, where will I go from here?

I am already at the end of my rope.

I wish to fall to my knees, to let my strength finally give out fully. My fingers long to press into the dirt, my magic asking me to wreak havoc upon this space to match my mood. The idea of turning back or continuing on is a dagger pressed against my throat, forcing me to choose.

I shake my head, clearing the negative voices from my mind.

I *will not* go back and I *will* create a new life for myself. I have unwoven my chains, finding the ability within myself to become *free.*

A figure opens the door to the cottage, a woman of my kind. She stands in the doorway, bathed in the golden light of her home. Her hair falls from around her shoulders like willow branches. She is soft and steady on her feet as she takes in my disgruntled figure.

There is no demand in her stance, no urgency. Just an empty question and an impending curiosity of who this forest might have dropped on her doorstep. She steps aside, creating an open door for me to walk through. Warmth from inside spills out into the night and I shiver, reminded of my lack of clothing for the winter sure to come.

I stand as still as possible, assessing my options. My throat is tight, words tangled inside of me.

Her eyes pierce my own and she nods just once, quickly, as if it did not happen at all. She leaves the door wide open but moves inside, as if leaving the decision fully up to me.

As if she would not blame me for turning around and deciding to leave.

There is empty space inside from what I can see. Space, just possibly, for *me.* It does not feel like a trap, like fragments of the prison I escaped. It is welcoming, inviting, calling out to me. A gentle wind gives me a shove from behind, as if propelling me forward.

I trust the earth to guide me. It would not lead me astray.

So I do.

I take a step. And another. The weight of the past falling off my shoulders as I step through the house's threshold and into this new place.

And I let the door shut behind me.

SHATTERED BLAME

I allow the fire within my hearth to die down to a single ember, unwilling to be consumed by its unrelenting heat any longer.

Even though it brings me back to that fateful day all those years ago.

Reject remembering. Move on.

It took me years to be willing to light kindling again. Even more so, to use my magic.

The air is crisp tonight, laced with a bitter cold that glitters on my windowpanes. Frost traces the edges, a delicate design creeping onto the glass like a silent whisper. As I sit and look out, my breath fogs the material, cold pressing into my skin and wrapping around me like an old, unwelcome memory.

I am no stranger to cold, my mate having been ice-gifted, but this chill seeps deep within my heart, matching my mood. My room is dim, only the pale light of the moon illuminating the walls surrounding me, casting long shadows across the worn wood floors.

Though I never would have believed it to be possible, this cottage truly became *home* to us. It's small, but sturdy - its walls thick with years of both good and bad times throughout my long life. Everything is aged, well-used. There are cracks in the beams, worn edges on the floors, no dust in sight - proof to how we truly *lived* here. That it is still standing is a testament to the lifetimes lived here and the moments we survived.

Together.

The scent of herbs - lavender, thyme, rosemary - linger in the air, grounding me to this moment in time. As I inhale as deep as I am able, my chest rattling in pain and effort, I cannot escape the scent of something else. All at once, recollection hits my senses. One of burnt wood, of smoke and ashes lingering in the air. It is the aroma of destruction to me - of overwhelming loss.

I cannot allow myself to wander there yet within my mind. No, first I must bind myself to the soft, quiet moments that came after. I must remind my body that a good life was lived. One full of beauty, of time spent well, of unexpected changes.

I flood my memories with thoughts of Eirwen, his presence a constant warmth beside me through it all. He was a steady anchor in the midst of everything that came to pass, picking up my broken pieces when I had no will left to live. His laughter, the way it would break me out in goosebumps, shivers running down my spine at the music hidden in the sound.

His hands were always gentle, caressing and guiding me toward this life together. Eirwen's mind was strong, allowing him to build this home together beam by beam after losing our first two cottages - creating a space that was once again ours. He helped me take back what *she* took from us.

And this house is a true reflection of our love.

For years, it was just him and I. But later in our journey, another joined, gifted to us by Elynia's forest. She was so full of wonder and life, just what we needed to bring light back into our final days. The way she'd run so freely outside, her carefree nature gifting us with a renewed sense of self.

Though her life before us was unbearable, she broke through the weight on her heart and learned to love again. She was a missing piece to a puzzle that we didn't know needed completed. She would not be contained by us and our town, though. She needed more from Elynia than that.

These moments keep me grounded, holding me together in these final times. Tonight, as I sit here alone, the ache of their absence weights so heavily on me. I never wanted to be the last one left. This was not supposed to be my burden to bear.

Not that I wanted it to be either of theirs.

The warmth of their presence feels like a distant dream, slipping through my fingers no matter how tightly I try to hold on.

I pull my cloak taut around my shoulders, the interwoven fabric soft against my skin, but it still does not shield me from the coldness within my own soul. I trace the edges of the worn cloth I knit together with my own hands, my fingers trembling slightly as the frayed threads remind me of how quickly things unravel.

Even the most delicate and tightly woven bonds can break when tested with the weight of time.

And in that moment, I stand amid a dying glow of our once-vibrant town. My heart is in my throat, fragile shards of sorrow encompassing me as I watch the flames consume everything I held dear. All because of *her*.

She stands at the edge of my memory, once my friend but now a stranger.

An enemy.

An innocent and ambitious heir to The Clyrn, she fell into my life at a moment I least expected. Growing close, like sisters, we shared our deepest secrets with the other, binding ourselves together in honor, truth, love. I remember that day with painful clarity: the gentle touch of her hands against mine, the whispered promises of unity between our own small world and Elynia's.

No more hiding for the people of The Clyrn, peace for the world itself. In that tender moment, I believed that our shared dream of prosperity could bridge the chasm of chaos within Elynia and beyond.

But as dusk fell that evening, and I found that she had departed sooner than planned, I began to hear the yells and screams of those around me. The string of treachery and betrayal floods me, shocking my system just as it did centuries ago. To her, it may have just been a single, unassuming choice: a slip of the tongue too early, an accidental confession.

For the rest of The Clyrn, though, that devastating mishap ignited within me both hatred and despair as our people were chased, caught, and killed.

Not her, though. No. It was later that I found out that she and her family had been spared.

A fool's bargain.

My eyes shut tightly, attempting to refrain from picturing an imaginary image I wish so desperately that I could erase: her voice spilling our secrets to those different from us, their eager hands reaching for our downfall, expressions blurred by greed and envy.

Though I was not there to witness her treachery firsthand, I was there for the ruination of all I had ever known and loved.

And because of her choices, the rest of us were turned to ash.

I drift through the decay of that day in my mind, hearing the echoes of our lost community. My skin feels the heat of those embers, soaring high into that dark night sky as a painful reminder of my trust so freely given and that she allowed it to go up in flames. The wind drifting in from the cracks of my house tastes of smoke and sorrow, whispering the names of those who perished, as if the earth itself mourns the beauty that was so ruthlessly extinguished.

And why wouldn't it? All we do is give to Elynia.
We do not take.

The despair threatens to overwhelm me, the taste in my mouth as bitter as the betrayal that ruined us. Though I know I need to relinquish my hold on the bitterness within me, I have carried it for far too long to easily depart with it now.

A wound that has never fully healed, a scar that I constantly trace in quiet moments when I am reminded that no one else carries the burden that I carry. The fire I once wielded, the flames that should have burned bright enough to protect those I loved… how they faltered, how they flickered out in the face of human greed and violence.

I still see their faces, glimpses of their weapons reaching for me as we hid - the walls of our homes burning relentlessly. The smoke choked the air, curling into a dark sky, carrying with it the ashes of life.

The blame I hold against them courses within me with the strength of fire I once manipulated. I could not save them. I could not stop the destruction that consumed our land.

I was not enough.

And now, though our town has been rebuilt over the ages, I still feel the echoes of silence that rang through the air after Eirwen and I emerged from the rubble of ruins. I feel a pinch at my palms, realizing I have been clenching my fists as I revisit these memories.

A gust of wind rattles the door, and the latch trembles. I lift my head, my breath catching in my throat at the violence happening outside my safe space. It's almost as if Elynia knows that my time nears. The cold grows much sharper, more defined. A light layer of snow swirls through the air, dancing like my fleeting memories.

The door is nudged open ever so slightly, a small nose emerging from beyond the threshold. My heart pangs once again as I gaze at my greatest gift.

Keeks.

She steps forward, recognition in her eyes. Her crystal form gleams under the moonlight, her fur refracting light in sharp, frozen angles. Oh, how I have missed her. I cannot believe she is here, back with me. A fog of a memory passes through my brain. We had lost her… that fateful day when everything changed.

When we failed them both.

How much more disappointment in my living will those around me be able to take? It is time for the gods to take me and deal me my fate.

As her eyes pierce mine, deep and knowing, she holds me captive. The years have stretched so painfully, so long - each one a reminder of everything I have tried so hard to bury beneath the weight of time. It's as if she knows exactly what I've been wrestling with, exactly what I might need in this moment.

She stands still, just as enchanting as she was then, and it is as if she never left us. If only Eirwen could see her now. I feel the bond between her and me, ringing harmoniously in my heart, as if she is still a part of me after all.

It dawns on me that it's possible she is not truly still here, but a gift from the universe to help me move on. When she was created, she was meant to last through our immortal years.

She was a companion, a protector, a friend. But tonight, her presence stirs something deep within me that I have been avoiding. Something locked away so deep in the dark corners of my heart that it might have to claw its way out.

Keeks steps forward, wispy at the edges as if a ghost, but still as graceful and sure as she always was. I reach out, ready to be met with her soft coat. The moment my hand brushes against her fur, a shock of relief floods my body. I close my eyes, allowing the chill of peace to settle deep within me. It does not burn, nor does it sting, but it soothes my soul. Somehow, it is a reflection of everything I have kept hidden inside of me.

Though she is a cold, frosted being, she now gifts me with warmth and comfort in impossible ways.

And still, she offers me a tenderness I do not deserve. I have lived the end days of my life in an edge of bitterness that my mate would not be proud of. He was always so much better, so much kinder, than I. Even then, his love never wavered, despite all the pain I laid at his feet.

I would not wish for him, or our people, to see me this way.

Keeks does not pull away, nor does she come any closer. She allows me a moment to hold onto her, to feel the weight of my grief without judgment. In that silence, I find something new there that I have not given myself before - permission.

Permission to mourn, but properly. Permission to remember, but peacefully. Permission to feel the depth of my loss in all areas. Not as a burden, or as a weight on my heart, but as a part of who I am and the journey I have been on all these years.

And maybe... I could learn to be grateful for that journey.
Every hill, every valley.

Forgiveness does not mean the wounds vanish, whether overnight or with time. No, it just means they stop bleeding.

The weight in my chest shifts, cracking open just enough for my breathing to loosen. Everything does not feel quite so sharp now, the memories fading to be a soft glow of love that endured through *every* hardship. My precious ice fox steps back, her eyes still on mine.

I hope she is proud of me. I long for her to go tell Eirwen that with his help, with *her* help, I have shattered the blame that I held within me for so long. And more than that, that I am ready to go - to see him again.

She turns, quickly disappearing into the night outside these four walls just as she appeared. Wisps of snow are left in her wake, a mere shadow of her presence just moments before, as if she was not really here at all.

The room is no longer suffocating, no longer consuming me. In the act of remembering the pain from the past, I have found a small space within myself to release it.

And for the first time in many, many years, I am not burdened wholly by what I lost. Instead, I am filled with an appreciation for what remains and what was rebuilt. For had the past not had its time, the present would not be as it is today.

What is left of me is love, even in its most fragile form.

And that is enough to carry me into the rising dawn.

GLIMPSES OF FROST

Some time ago, before everything within Elynia changed...

I was not created to be still.

I slip through the trees, snow making up my very essence. My paws leave no mark, wind itself carrying me far. My spirits are lifted, a day spent outside leaving me breathless and exhilarated. I glance back briefly, expecting to be followed, but company is not something I come across often.

Glimpses of frost lies untouched in front of me, just out of reach. Elynia is quieter than I've witnessed before. The sky is an endless color of indigo, scattered with stars that glisten like the ice I'm made of. Snow drapes from the branches above, heavy and new, the air crisp with my favorite scent - winter.

I am a creature of ice, cold and constant, and I have no need for anything beyond what I already have. I know my purpose. I am a guardian, a gift, a symbol of promises between two bound hearts - my Makers. From the moment I was created, I understood what my duties would be: I can roam, I can seek, I can freely leave. It is up to me to choose whether to remain by their side, or to return at the end of everyday.

Without fail, I come back to my family every dusk.

Though I long to explore the rest of Elynia, I know there are no others like me out there. Home is where I am meant to stay - curled up in their large bed, sitting in the presence of our fire.

It is most of what I've ever known, and I do not mind the routine. Still, sometimes, I cannot help that curiosity gets the better of me.

There is just *so much* out there.

The cottage is small, but it is *ours*. Each crack in the walls, each faded beam speaks of times well spent. We live our lives carefully, finding refuge in each other. They care for me as I care for them, though their affection has become lax as of late.

I'm sure it is just the years weighing on them.

I've never known any other life. I am a fixture here, and I carry those duties in an unquestioning, unrelenting way. I exist because of their love, and I must repay them with my loyalty.

The unknown lies before me, just as it always has. Flurries of snow fall all around me and I chase their small forms, bounding through and yipping at the chilly air. Flashes of nights past play in my mind repeatedly when I wander from the cottage for too long. Memories on the edge of my brain: ones of being curled up in darkness, my fur shimmering in the glow of firelight.

I chase away the frost, just as I often run from burning embers, constantly having to dart away from flickers of warmth that send ripples of water down my spine. My oldest friend, my only friend - always twirling away from me in its own space, as if daring me to keep my distance.

I always do.

Perhaps it is some cruel joke of our Makers to have created us in opposition, unable to fully understand and be with the other. Maybe I was made to unravel in her glow, each flicker daring me to avoid who she really is.

Longing plagues me. I wake in the early hours of the morning, long before dawn, just to run in the cold wind and feel it tug at the edge of my fur. The world outside *calls* to me, a vast and wild place filled with stretched skies, looming forests, and plains untouched. I cannot help but yearn for the freedom beyond the four cottage walls.

But still, at the end of the day, I am always drawn back to the hearth, to the heat that relents at dusk, the warmth that ties me to this family.

They love me. They need me. I remind myself of that, over and over. I was made to be the balance between us, to reflect the care and curiosity they hold within their hearts. It is my duty to stay for *them.*

I can't help that the world outside tugs at me. There are so many whispered stories told to me through the wind, so many places I could roam were I truly free. A distant adventure might await, one that is wholly my own.

A place where I could be more.

And some days, I crave my fire's presence in these winter woods. How I wish she could run and play with me, weaving through the trees with care and expertise. She might dare me to follow her, leaving trails of smoldering foliage in her wake. I would have bound after her in delight, if that meant I would not be alone out here.

I can sense her from here, even now.

It feels... different.

I tremble, but not from the bitter cold seeping into my fur. Though we are two entirely opposite beings, we belong beside the other.

The forest hushes, Elynia's shadows stretching longer as the day ends.

I have always belonged to someone. First, to my Maker, then

to his lover, who lets me curl up at her feet and lean in close to her touch. But more than that, I belong to my fire, who was created in tandem with me. It is her tether I feel pulling me back to the cottage tucked away in Elynia's forest.

There are no voices calling out my name, but my heart still responds.

I have not heard my name in so long, I might have forgotten what it sounds like.

As I make my way back, my heart begins to feel unusually empty. A day spent exploring typically leaves me light, but briefly frustrated. It is as if everyday, my world waits to begin again, and just as it does, I must decide to stop it from happening.

The light layer of snow on the ground beneath my feet is undisturbed, a pristine covering of white. I leap forward, spiraling through the frost-laced air, the crunch of ice beneath me and around me. The cold does not bite, and the wind does not hinder me. I press my paws into the solid dirt, but there is no give. I leave no imprint. The surface remains smooth and glistening under the rising moon's pale light.

A whisper moves through the frosted tips of bushes, curling around me like a breath. The trees stand in silence, as if alerting me something is coming. Maybe Elynia is hoping I will stay this time.

But I can't.

I stretch, not far from home now. The moon finds itself in the night sky, the stars blinking overhead as if watching me. The beginning of winter begins to stir around me, creatures of all kinds finding a space to rest and hide. I close my eyes - not to disappear, but to feel where my feet are.

To listen.

What should my next step be? To run? To move? To *be free?*
Where does the frost and wind long to take me?

What if I had no cottage to return to, no community nor family to fall back on? Would I mourn? Or would that free me to live how I long to? Are our bonds not meant to be lived in - wholly felt - not clutched? Maybe I am not meant to stay here forever.

We meet, we dance, we part. That is the nature of all things, isn't it? The cycle we are all captivated by and tethered to. When the time has come, we let go. We do not hold onto what will become ash on the wind and smoke in the sky.

We release.

Letting go is not the same as forgetting. It is an act of trust, a moment of understanding. I do not need to stay with them to know that what we have is tangible and *matters.* Perhaps, in leaving, I might honor what we have more than if I were to cling to things of the past. I do not need to prove to myself and Elynia that we are *real.*

I linger by our cottage door, paws pressed against the cool wood. I can feel my fire from here, warmth bleeding out into the exterior. The hearth crackles softly, my ears picking up even the quietest of sounds.

Quieter than usual, somehow.

An unease lingers within those four walls. My fur prickles, alerting me that change is coming.

Am I ready to face it?

Our Makers have spoken of things I do not fully understand - of war, unrest, of others of their kind banding together. There is fear in their words, but something greater than that too. *Excitement* for what is to come. They need me now, more than ever. They need my steadiness, my quiet presence, my guidance.

Could that be what this is?

And yet, the outside world pulls at me even stronger.

I am torn between two loves. How could I possibly choose?

A weight on my chest stumps my breathing. To stay is not a command. But what will I leave behind if I go?

I face the closed door, beckoning at me to open it and peer inside. To discover what is happening within this cottage. What will I find if I stay?

Hesitancy grips at me. I think of the warmth of my fire, the comfort it provides to all of us. I was made to stay with it - this is *who I am*. The weight of my duties press down on me, a heavy blanket of expectation that I am afraid I cannot meet.

My fire's flames call to me, almost, and I think of her - unaware of the turmoil within me. If I leave, if I choose to roam, I would lose her and our Makers. I would lose everything that has ever made me feel whole, everything that has ever given me purpose.

But I want to be out here instead.

My heart twists at the thought of forsaking them and leaving them behind.

I nudge the door open with my nose, padding silently across the room. My paws barely make a sound on the chilled floor. The atmosphere in here tonight is different - colder. I jump in the rocking chair in the corner, my favorite spot.

Perhaps it will bring me some comfort.

Or some answers.

The winter wind funnels in through the window next to me, rustling my fur the way I love that it does.

I curl up, closing my eyes, imagining the world outside waiting for me. Beyond the boundaries of this cottage, beyond the heat of the fire. I see snowflakes falling from the sky, beckoning me forward. I feel the magic of it all around me, seeping into my bones and heart. I skate across ice forming on lakes and rivers. Elynia is vast, and beautiful, and I could be part of it all if I choose to walk away.

My labored breaths come loose in a deep sigh. For now, I will stay. Perhaps someday, I might be awarded the chance to live a life of my own. One day, the wind will not let me go. Someday, I will step out of this world with my fire and my Makers and I will *not* hesitate to take what is being offered to me freely.

I settle deeper into the cushions of this chair, the air still uneasy.

Change is coming. I will not pursue it, or chase after it relentlessly. Instead, I will wait for it and let it find *me*.

And when it does, I will be ready.

Sneak Peek…

Read on for a sneak peak of Macayla Dawn's debut YA novel, *The Mountain's Crown* (book one in the Fated Paths Duology).

The Mountain's Crown

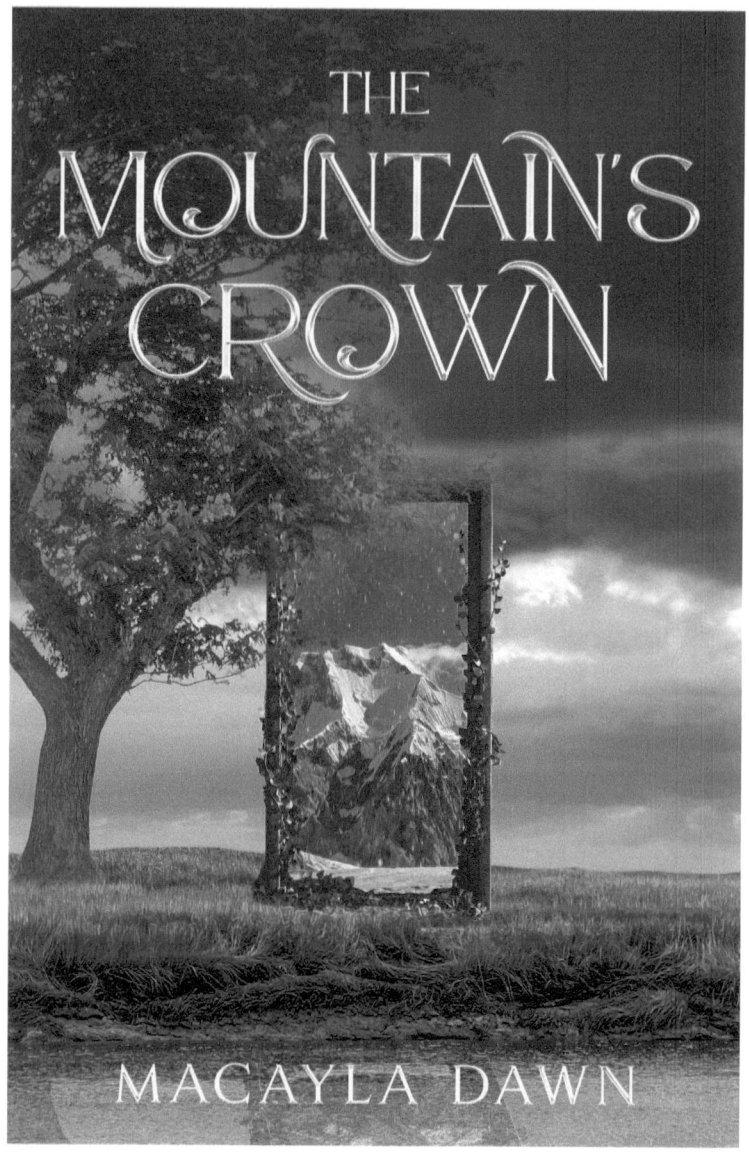

ONE

I could write poems regarding her beauty.

She was the most stunning person I'd ever laid eyes on. The golden touch of her skin seeped into my thoughts like a warm summer day. Her brown eyes held answers to questions I didn't know I needed to ask. Her dark hair wrapped around my dreams like a lover's caress. Her laughter flitted through my mind like a song on the wind.

But she is not mine.

And I will never have her.

TWO

To be drawn to light is to feel alive.

To bask in the warmth of the sun is to feel at home.

Unfortunately for me, Paralia has not felt like home in a long time. Ever since my teenage years, I have longed to experience something new. I have begged the sun to hide, so that I may experience the touch of rain on my skin, or the bite of cold air upon my nose.

And yet, the sun does not give in. Day after day, my bright star shows up and asks me to drown in its rays. My only reprieve is the night sky and the coolness that evening brings.

So here I am, stuck laying on these sandy shores of Paralia, recharging my soul the only way I know how - allowing the sun to soak into my heart and skin.

⛰ ⛰ ⛰

"P! I've been looking everywhere for you."

Squinting my eyes open, I turn my head toward the voice coming to sit next to me.

"Cal, don't act like you didn't know I was here." I resume laying on my back with my face toward the sun. Callious and I just chatted not even an hour ago about where I would be spending the day. Truthfully, he purposefully likes to push my buttons.

All of a sudden, the feel of sand coats my body as he throws mounds onto me.

TWO

"Cal!" I giggle and rush upright, trying to spit the sand out of my mouth and brush it off my face. "What has gotten into you?"

"Oh no, I can't believe I got sand on you! I suppose that means we need to take a swim to get it off?" He lifts an eyebrow at me and pastes a smirk on that stupid tan face of his.

Now that I'm sitting up and able to look him in his sea-green eyes, I see that he has shown up to *my* spot in shorts made for swimming.

"We have dinner tonight - I can't swim today and you know that!" I laugh and smack his arm. Cal stands and offers me a hand, but as I gain my footing and take it, he tackles me to the ground and shoves sand in my dark hair. "Callious!"

"Now you've ruined it, Nelly. I wasn't going to, but I am now required to insist you go on a swim with me. You wouldn't want to head back home plastered with sand, would you?"

Scowling, I push out of his grasp.

"I assume you're expecting me to jump in with my dress on? I'll drown, if that's what you want."

"You should know me better than that by now." Cal grabs his messenger bag slung around his shoulder and whips out a deep green two-piece tank and shorts set. "Tailored just for you for these warm waters. You ran out of the palace before I could give it to you."

"This is stunning - you shouldn't have!" I squeal as I hold the piece up to me. This may be the most beautiful thing I own, with gold detailing on the seams. "Where did you find this?"

"It was Eva's from years ago. She told me she knew of a seamstress who could give it a new life. I just got it back from her this morning."

Grasping the fabric, my smile drops with that declaration.

Such a precious gift, and of course it had to come secondhand through my sister first. I shouldn't be upset, it's still the prettiest set I've ever seen.

"So, does this mean a swim is in order?" He wags his eyebrows at me. Huffing, I roll my eyes in response.

"Give me five minutes to change, and we will race to the waters. And I will not be going easy on you this time."

⌂ ⌂ ⌂

Five minutes later, give or take a few, we are shoulder to shoulder facing the Neronian Sea. Even though the name of our sea means cruel, or barbarous, I can assure you it is anything but. I have never experienced warmer, calmer waters than those to the west of Paralia.

I look over my shoulder to my oldest friend. Callious and I have been out here more times than I can count, but for some reason, this time feels different. Maybe it's the way his eyes are shining brighter than normal, or the way he stands so confidently next to me, but I can feel an energy radiating off him that is addicting.

"Ready?" I ask.

"Ready!" He whips his eyes to meet mine. Years of friendship and a mutual understanding reflect in his sea-green eyes. I suppose that could be why looking at the Neronian is one of my favorite views - it reminds me of my best friend.

Deviously, we smile at each other. My heart is pounding out of my chest as I make sure my feet are planted firm in the shifting sand.

"GO!"

We run toward the coastline, elbowing and pushing our way past each other. Years of racing the other means that we have become equal in almost every way, knowing just how fast our opponent is and where they may fall.

My right foot careens into a divot in the sand and I stumble, but Cal is right there to grab my arm and make sure I'm able to keep going. Even though we are competing, he will never let me fall too far behind.

Our feet meet the cerulean waters as we splash past the shallow part and start swimming toward the waist-deep current. Laughing, he tries to push my head under, but I grab his wrist and attempt to push him over instead.

My body is exhausted, but the race was exhilarating. The warm sea caresses my lean figure as I lay back to wash the sand off. Somehow, Cal always knows exactly what I need.

He dunks his head below the surface and flings his dark hair around as he comes back up, coating me in the salty sea. Laughing, I push him further away from me.

"I absolutely won that race. What will I get for being first?"

"You're delusional if you believe you won that. But, I suppose that's something I already knew since you still choose to be friends with me after all this time." He winks and dives under as he starts to swim toward me. Suddenly, there are hands around my waist.

I screech as he begins to throw me over his shoulder. "Callious! Put me down!"

"If you insist, princess." He throws me away from him as if I'm only a sack of vegetables, and into the surf beneath us. I hit the bottom of the sea, and rushed back up for a breath, only to find him doubled over laughing so hard he can't keep his eyes open.

"I'm not sure why I allow myself to be treated like this by you. Maybe I've had enough!" I shove him with my elbow while wringing out my dripping wet hair. This is going to take forever to dry now before dinner tonight.

"The day you've had enough of me will be the day I die, Penelope." He smiles as he shoves me back. "Thank you for allowing me to be here today with you, P. I hope I made it worth your while."

I shrug as I say, "I suppose the swim wasn't the most terrible idea you've ever had." Winking at him, I begin to swim back toward the shore where my clothes and responsibilities await. "This has been a fantastic day. Thank you for coming out here."

Halting me, he grabs my ankles and pulls me back in to spin around and face him. Lifting my eyes, I give him a questioning look. "What?"

He sheepishly smiles as he runs a hand through his hair. "Happy birthday, Nelly. I hope I can make twenty-one as special for you as you are to me."

My hand finds my heart and I give him a sad smile back. "You're the only one that has remembered. Thank you."

He pulls me in for a hug. As we turn back to make our way back to the beach, he flings his arm around my shoulder and kisses the top of my head.

"I know." He murmurs into my hair.

Yes, better than anyone in my life, he knows.

THREE

We hurry back to the palace, noting the high tide beginning to rise and fall beneath the brick columns that hold my home high above sea level.

One gated wall and fifty-two stairs later, my legs are burning as I rush into my bedroom.

Grabbing a towel, I begin wringing my wet strands through the coarse fabric. I put heat on my hair this morning for the first time in a year, but the saltwater always brings out my natural curls.

Huffing in annoyance, I finish drying my long locks as best as possible. If I hurry, I'll have just enough time to change and make it back down to the dining room.

Scouring my wardrobe for something simple to slip on, I quickly find my favorite dress. I'm aware that tonight is important, but I truthfully have no idea what is being announced or what might be going on.

I can't help but twirl in the mirror and admire the light pink sheer layer that adorns the maroon skirt. My sleeves are billowed toward the middle but fit tight at my wrists, and my neckline hearts over my chest. I cannot believe my sister, Ana, tired of the dress so quickly. I was ecstatic to take it off her hands.

Slipping into pink flats, I head down the hall to our dining room with just a few minutes to spare.

◒ ◒ ◒

I place my hands in my lap as I'm seated and take a deep breath. It's not easy being without Callious in situations like this, where he cannot be the calm to the storm raging inside of me. Regardless of whether or not anyone else here actually sees me, I know he always does.

Tapping on a glass, my father rises and begins dinner.

"Frey, please join me in standing as I introduce our guest for the evening."

Following my family to our feet, I survey the room. My gaze catches on the wide wooden doors that align the wall to our backs. Opening, they present a man with an aura of cool arrogance walking toward us with purpose. His head is held high, and the silver crown atop his head gives off an edge of bitter cold.

This man smiles as he reaches his place next to my father at the end of our table. Looking toward us with ice-blue eyes, I begin to notice many of my siblings' jaws have dropped. It appears the only one holding himself together is Everett, though that is no surprise.

"Thank you for welcoming me into Paralia. It is an honor to set foot once again on your warm coast. Though, I do prefer my air with a subtle chill to it." He chuckles.

"You are always welcome here. It has been many years since we last saw each other, so allow me to reintroduce the Frey to you. First, my Queen, Briar." Father takes Mother's hand and presents it to this man. His name is on the tip of my tongue, but I cannot seem to place him as my siblings have. There's something in his sharp features that is making me feel as though I've been here before.

"Next, my heir. Prince Everett, please present yourself and

be seated."

Everett faces our guest and bows deeply. After carefully finding his seat, he brings his eyes back to our father's.

"The twins, Ana and Eva, please present yourselves and be seated."

They do the same, as is custom. Down the line, my father goes: to Finneus, Leila, and Carter, until he reaches me.

"And my youngest, Pen. Please present yourself and be seated."

Trying not to huff in annoyance at the nickname, I follow in my family's steps and make eye contact with our guest, curtsying low to the ground. Bowing my head, I rise and find my seat. Once my eyes are back on my father, all nine of us raise our drinking glasses toward the ceiling in tandem.

"I am the Frey." My father states, still standing.

"And we are the Frey." We respond, taking a sip out of our glasses and placing them back on the table in unison.

"Well, that was a very cute show you put on there, Zannan. Your family has certainly grown in the years we've spent in strife."

I cannot help myself - my eyes grow wide. I have never heard someone speak so casually to my father. Even my mother would not dare use such a tone.

Who is this man?

Father only laughs back as he sits and replies, "Surely you are not still in denial that it was your Kingdom that caused this rift between us in the first place, Kori."

Kingdom.
Kori.
Strife.
Curse the sun above - this is Oresteia's King.

"It's very unfortunate that you do not know how to take responsibility for your actions. I do hope that Prince Everett is able to steer from your direction in that area should he go on to become King." Kori makes a pointed look toward my brother while taking a drink from his glass. Somehow, he looks as if he is at home here at our table. He lounges back on his seat as if it's his own throne.

Everett clears his throat and looks toward our father for permission to speak. With a subtle nod of his head, Everett declares:

"It would be an honor to take after my King in every aspect once I'm able to receive a crown of my own."

Kori waves his hand in the air and brings it down hard on our table, making me jump.

"Let's cut to the chase, Zannan. I would prefer not to have to stay for dinner if I can help it. Your seafood is…" He pauses to think. "Lusterless, to say the least. Now, give me what has been taken, or give me the girl."

All seven of our heads whip toward my father. My mother sits at his right, and she is the only one who does not look surprised at what is conspiring between these two. Silence overwhelms our space as my father and King Kori stare daggers at each other.

Ana is the one who chooses to break the silence. "My King, if I may, I believe we are all a bit lost regarding what King Kori just proclaimed."

My father looks toward her with softer eyes.

"Thank you for asking, Ana. Attendants, please clear the room for the rest of the evening."

Feet scurry as our servers and workers race out of the doors as fast as possible. Unfortunately, it does not appear as if we will be eating dinner anytime soon. As if on cue, my stomach lets out an embarrassing growl.

Carter kicks my foot from under the table and sneaks me a pointed smirk. Blushing, I grab my glass and take a slow sip of the fizzy drink, hoping it will curb my appetite for the time being.

Once the doors have sealed and the room consists of only the ten of us, my father stands once more.

"King Kori Pan of Oresteia has declared his intentions to go to war on Paralia. He is under the impression that the Frey stole something of extreme value to their Kingdom. Should we not return the item tonight, which I have assured King Kori that we do not have," a pointed look passes between them, "we will then be forfeiting our rights to decline this looming war."

Before any of us can chime in, my mother adds, "Zannan, tell them of the other condition."

My father's shoulders droop ever so slightly as he sighs and continues.

"Because I cannot convince Oresteia's King to reverse his declaration of war, I have negotiated to send an ambassador of Paralia to Oresteia until the season's change to give us time to look for this stolen item.

"This ambassador will give Oresteia insight into Paralia and our systems to help heal the rift that began between our Kingdoms long ago. Should this item not be found at the end of this season, war will begin."

The air is thick with shock as we process the words my father just spoke. Six weeks feels like such a short time in hindsight.

How are we supposed to look for this stolen item when it's clear we don't know what the artifact is?

Kori smirks from his seat. "Don't leave out the best part,

Zannan. Tell them who's going back with me."

Our gazes snap back to my father's.

His old, stubborn eyes meet my own while his hand finds my mother's.

"Penelope."

Acknowledgments

Round two of publishing a book is here already, and it's been a wild ride. This book, world, the characters and themes were not on my radar at *all* for this year. So first, truly, I'd like to thank the short story contest from which *Whispers of Ash* was born. Honestly, that seven day challenge is where this entire collection began.

There are a lot of topics we as people don't love to talk about. Loss, change, nostalgia, losing friends, leaving toxic places, longing for freedom in different capacities, feeling like a stranger in your own skin. All of those things feel uncomfortable to address, usually making those who so deeply relate to these topics feel alone and as if they don't belong. So I thought, what better way to address these internal, soul crushing issues than to wrap it up in a cozy fantasy world that's easy to digest and understand?

Long story short, I hope Elynia and the characters within it made you feel like you *do* belong somewhere. Because you so desperately do!

This book wouldn't have been possible without many individuals, many who were mentioned in my first book, and even some who I've only recently met and connected with since moving to a new state. As time continues and as life changes, I'm thankful that some people and things never do.

First, of course, my Savior. Next to Him is the only place that really matters.

Second, Hunter. Thank you for encouraging me to take this dream full time and doing everything you can to make that happen. Writing this time around was much less dramatic, much less dire of a time in our marriage, but you have stayed my best friend through it all. Thank you for being my assistant at all my new "author events" and for choosing me.

To my families once again - you have always been behind me, for me, and with me. I love you so much!

Next, to my new friends and church family here in Indiana. What a community we have been blessed with! You all make me feel like I belong. Thank you.

Last, to you, my reader! I cannot believe you chose to pick up this book and read it in its entirety. Whether this is your first book of mine or you came from *The Mountain's Crown,* just know that I am so grateful for you. You are welcome here.

Reading is both a safe space and a home to my heart and I hope you find delight and rest in the words of these pages.

I can never thank you all enough,
    Macayla Dawn

About the Author

Macayla Dawn is a reader first and a writer second.

Growing up, she found herself drawn to worlds filled with demigods, fae, mystery and magic. The characters on those pages became more than just words in a book – they became friends. She is passionate about Jesus, grammar, fantasy, creativity, and ice cream.

In her free time, she loves to read (duh!), write, and explore different ways to express her creativity in all she does. She stays active through tennis, pickleball, working out, and walks with her husband and their dog. She loves to soak up the sun and host gatherings of all sorts.

Originally from Southeast Kansas, she now lives her dream life in Indiana.

Be sure to follow her bookstagram: @authormacayladawn.

Photograph taken by Every Little Thing Creative.

You can connect with me on:
- https://www.macayladawn.com
- https://www.instagram.com/authormacayladawn

Also by Macayla Dawn

Looking for more fantasy from this author?

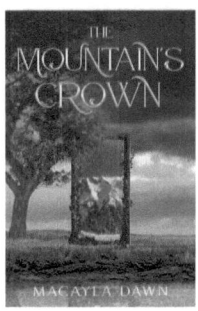

The Mountain's Crown
https://www.macayladawn.com/shop/p/themountainscrown
The choice is hers… But what if she didn't have to choose?

When twenty-one-year-old Penelope Frey is chosen to travel to Oresteia, her coastal Kingdom's rival land, she must put aside her life's wishes to search for what has been presumably stolen. Now surrounded by Oresteia's cold exterior, Penelope discovers their Kingdoms are on the brink of collapsing.

As Penelope strives to save her Kingdom, she finds herself trapped between two worlds. Can she recover what they claim she stole? Or will she doom their worlds into nonexistence?

The Mountain's Crown is a gripping tale filled with ambition, magic, betrayal, and redemption. This captivating story of resilience and discovery is author Macayla Dawn's debut novel in a new, breathtaking fantasy series: *The Fated Paths Duology*.

www.ingramcontent.com/pod-product-compliance
Ingram Content Group UK Ltd.
Pitfield, Milton Keynes, MK11 3LW, UK
UKHW042000230426
12048UKWH00009B/459